I0671881

# The Occulting Light

## Stories

Robert McDermott

RIVERSONG
BOOKS

An Imprint of Sulis International Press
Los Angeles | Dallas | London

THE OCCULTING LIGHT: STORIES
Copyright ©2024 by Robert McDermott. All rights reserved.

Versions of these stories have been published as follows: *The Moons of Gemini* first appeared in Memento Mori. *On Cornado Beach* and *Sukie in the Graveyard* first appeared in INOTE magazine. *Yours Ever, Erica* first appeared in Wicked Shadow Press Culture Cult Anthology. *When Insects Were as Big as Birds* and *Boats Against the Currents* first appeared in Crossways Magazine. *The Ghosts of Devil's Den* first appeared in ResAliens Zine. *The Headless Men of the Nahanni Valley* first appeared in Dear Booze. *6EQUJ5, Thank You Very Much!* was originally published by Riversong Press as part of their 2022 short story anthology. *Mossy Brennan's Road to Damascus* first appeared in Shorter Stories. *The Enormous Cat* first appeared in Pen and Paws. *The Fawn* first appeared in Rosette Malificarum.

Cover art: *Cold Mountain* by Michelle Owen

ISBN (print): 978-1-958139-35-6
ISBN (eBook): 978-1-958139-36-3

Published by Riversong Books
An Imprint of Sulis International
Los Angeles | Dallas | London

www.sulisinternational.com

# Contents

*The life of the dead is placed in the memory of the living.*

—*Cicero*

# THE MOONS OF GEMINI

As far as steady, uncomplicated, work went, schools were perfect. They paid well and while the money was nice, Turner enjoyed the modest, professional respect most of all. Private shoots often involved private dramas. Turner lost count of the unhappy kids he'd told to smile on account of their parents squabbling and fussing in pursuit of a perfect moment of family joy. These were bad, but the photography enthusiast who loitered and made bland observations about the set-up was worst of all. They'd ask what type of lens and film Turner used and so on. The intrusive presence would rattle on about the latest trends and insinuate their expertise was on a par with Turner's. Turner wouldn't engage them and eventually, they'd wander off.

In recent years, he'd had fewer and fewer recommendations and even fewer callbacks. Schools paid the bills and there was plenty of work, though it was mostly confined to the start of the school year, which made balancing the budget precarious at times. He didn't complain.

As he set up his umbrellas in the hall, a group of eager onlookers gathered. He moved around the space, looking through various cameras he'd brought to gauge the light. To add to the sense of fun, he'd take a few quick snaps of the crowd. The kids, who he guessed were mostly under ten, smiled and laughed and covered their faces or made funny faces. They stuck out their tongues and giggled. This behaviour prompted their teacher to tell them to stop being such a nuisance.

'It's no problem,' said Turner.

'They're just a little excited,' said their teacher apologetically.

Turner regarded her with interest. She was slim with short dark hair and was dressed in the efficient, modest elegance he'd so often seen among female teachers of a certain age. His eyes moved to her hands. He lifted the camera to his eye and took her picture. Her body was slightly in profile, and she didn't notice him taking the picture. Turner believed the most natural photographs happened when the subject was caught unaware. It was rare to find such a moment when the mask of social interaction was removed.

A bell rang and Turner watched the woman herd the kids from the hall with the organised calm of a sheepdog. As she disappeared through the doors, she looked over her shoulder. This time she caught him taking her picture. He thought he saw the flicker of a coy smile on her lips.

The morning was a slow procession of individual kids and class groups. They were all well turned out. Turner knew it was a race against time. Well-dressed and clean kids didn't stay that way for too long. The younger kids were a bit of a chore but mostly good fun. They wouldn't sit still, they reacted to the lights and anything else which distracted them, usually waving to their friends or looking off into the distance.

Occasionally, if it was a big job, Turner brought his friend Ian to help with the set-up, but Ian and his wife were in family court. Turner couldn't understand why people got married. He'd watched his parents sink into drink and denial. About half the family shoots he'd done were disrupted by trivial frustrations which culminated in someone, usually the father, losing their temper. These moments reminded him of his parents. He felt their malaise hung on him like a stale odour.

By lunchtime, the heavy work was done and Turner, not wanting to eat at the school, walked to a nearby pub. The military precision of working in schools was fine, but Turner didn't care too much for teachers. He found them far too orientated towards small talk.

In the pub, he ate a sandwich and drank a beer. He was photographing the staff after lunch and didn't care if they smelled booze on him. Sure, didn't some of them smell the same?

The school's headmaster, a cheerful red-faced man from Cork, with a paternal manner and big hands, laughed frequently. The ever-present threat of a jocular clap on the back made Turner uneasy.

'My young lad loves taking pictures with his phone,' said the headmaster as he directed the staff into their seats like a conductor arranging his orchestra.

'He took a great one of the sunset the other evening, it was marvellous.'

Turner smiled politely.

'He has a phone with a load of pixels, it's very good, so I hear.'

'Some phones have good cameras,' said Turner.

'Pixels are the things that make the picture, is that right?'

'They're a component of the image resolution,' said Turner, but the headmaster didn't hear him.

'How's that for you?' said the headmaster, 'arranged like sheep in a pen.'

Turner nodded, and once the headmaster sat, he made some rearrangements. Finally, he stood back, took in the entire frame before clicking his camera repeatedly. Once the shoot was done, he took a quick look through the digital images and was dismayed to see an orb. He zoomed in and saw it was floating in the space immediately above the woman whose picture he'd taken earlier. He scanned back through the other pictures of her. There was an orb in each one. It was a minor inconvenience. While his rational brain knew they were probably caused by the flash reflecting off dust particles, or water spots on the lens or even a defect in the camera, thoughts about how some people believed they were ghosts intruded into his mind. Orbs plagued his work over the years. He'd first noticed the phenomenon about twenty years before, while working for *The Independent*. He was in his apartment trying to figure out how to use low-level lighting most effectively. He took about a dozen pictures of himself in a mirror. While processing the images, he noticed a single, unmistakable orb floating above his left shoulder in every picture.

'It's nothing,' said his editor, 'something up with the camera or the light. We can brush it out.'

'It's called backscatter,' said a colleague, 'dust and things in the air.'

Turner, relatively youthful and in the company of senior, hard-drinking, journalists and photographers, felt awkward. He didn't want to be there, but etiquette demanded it.

'I heard it's ghosts,' said a tall man named Price, his voice heavy with insincerity.

A chorus of guffaws followed the comment.

'Ghosts,' someone snorted, 'what nonsense. It's a feeble mind that believes in ghosts.'

Turner's memory scuttled into the recesses of his mind. So much of his life and identity hid there in the darkness, only occasionally coming into the light when triggered by something in the real world. The sound of his parents arguing usually followed chatter of ghosts and orbs.

*Nonsense* thought Turner.

He began to pack away his equipment in the slow, deliberate ritual he'd created over the years. He was far away in thought. The woman from earlier was speaking to him.

'I'm sorry,' said Turner, 'I was miles away.'

'I'm Ms. Fallon,' said the woman offering her hand, 'Debbie.'

Turner felt a chill move through his chest. She stood still and, not wanting to make the situation any more uneasy, he shook her hand, it was soft but cold.

'Joe Turner.'

'Like the painter.'

'Like the painter,' he echoed.

Sometimes people commented on his name. It was usually followed with a comment about visiting the exhibition in The National Gallery. Turner didn't know how to handle small talk. It was like a fish in his hands, slippery and unwelcome, longing to return to its natural environment.

'My husband paints.'

Turner smiled. He continued to pack away equipment.

'I see you're busy, so I'll get straight to the point,' said Debbie, 'it's my daughter's birthday this weekend, she's ten, and I'd like you to take some pictures, a family portrait, maybe.'

Turner finished packing an umbrella into a box. His first instinct was to decline the request, but for some reason he couldn't reconcile with thought, he agreed.

'Great, may I have your card so we can make arrangements?'

Turner gave her his card and she smiled broadly before leaving him to finish packing up.

He scratched his cheek. He felt displaced and wondered why he'd so easily agreed to her. What had compelled him, was it reason or emotion, he couldn't figure it out which part of him had been persuaded. It was as if someone had blown away the dust in his soul and found something underneath, an image perhaps, though he couldn't tell what shape it took.

Later, while he processed the photos from the day's shoot, he found his mind wandering to his own school years. The quiet of his lab often provoked this kind of thought. Though almost everything was digital, he still enjoyed using silver chloride and silver iodide. Immersing photographic paper in the solution and waiting for the image to emerge was a meditative process. As Debbie's image emerged from the blank photographic paper, he took pride in how he'd captured the expression on her face. He admired how clear the fine imperfections of her skin were. In the black and white image, she appeared more alive and real than anything a digital image could render. He lifted the paper from the tray and hung it on a line to dry. The orb over her shoulder was there, he knew as soon as the picture began to surface it would be. He also knew it was in human nature to find patterns and meanings in things which didn't possess them. It was called apophenia, and it belonged to Turner's rational vocabulary. What he couldn't shake, or perhaps didn't want to, was the thought of how she might have appeared as a child.

*

The following Saturday, he arrived for the shoot about ten minutes earlier than expected. The previous night's drinking woke him early. He took a walk to shake the roughness from his head. He'd been mulling over the orbs in the photos, vacillating between acceptance of what they could be and dismissal of what surely wasn't true.

He parked a short distance from the house. It was like most other suburban homes. There was nothing distinct with which to work with at the front. It faced north, which meant there'd be good light to the rear. Debbie told him there was space in the back garden and a few trees for texture. She didn't want anything special, just something tasteful to mark the occasion and please the grandparents. Turner told her he didn't do parties and asked if there'd be other kids there. She reassured him any visitors would be arriving after the shoot was finished.

As he approached the house, he took a few casual pictures. The day was brightening, and the sun danced along the house's exterior in an interesting way. The front door opened, and a broad-shouldered man stepped out.

'You must be Joe.'

Turner nodded.

'I'm Chris,' said the man, offering his hand.

They shook hands.

'That looks like it's been around the block,' said Chris, looking intently at the camera hanging from Turner's neck.

'It's my first camera. A gift from long ago.'

Chris nodded in appreciation and invited Turner inside.

As they moved into the kitchen, Turner was impressed by the decor. The colour scheme, arrangement of furniture and framed pictures gave the interior a sense of warmth. This was clearly a home. The kitchen area was a riot of sunlight. There were three Velux windows in an angular roof built around the original wood frame of the eaves. The kitchen, however, was not warm. Everything was white. The breakfast bar, the chairs, the cabinets. The walnut floor provided a note of contrast and the hanging ferns a note of colour, but the room reminded Turner of an operating theatre's stringent sterility.

Debbie emerged from the back garden. Accompanying her was a girl who stopped Turner's breath. He had to suppress a gasp and felt a rare, troubling wave of emotion pour over him. The girl, perhaps sensing something, moved in close to her mother.

'It's a lovely day,' said Debbie smiling, 'thanks so much for making the time.'

'I'm happy to,' said Turner.

He tried not to look at the girl, but his eyes moved towards her as if being pulled by magnets. Debbie laughed.

'Don't be shy, this is the man who's going to take your picture.'

'I'm Joe.'

The girl's face was tight and hard, as if there was nothing behind her eyes.

'Her name is Anna, and she's not normally this shy,' said Debbie.

Chris made a pot of coffee and put a cup in front of Turner. Turner thanked him and put it to his lips. It was hot and bitter, and the aroma reminded him of how booze and coffee lingered on his father's breath and clothes.

'Have you a family?' asked Chris.

Debbie tried to make light of the unsolicited personal question by suggesting Chris was a naturally curious person who sometimes forgot his manners.

'No, not anymore,' said Turner, 'my parents are dead.'

'Sorry to hear that,' said Debbie.

'You're an only child?' said Chris.

Turner didn't respond, and Chris didn't press the question.

After coffee, Turner and Chris stepped into the back garden while Debbie and Anna got changed. The garden was wide and shallow. The trees Debbie described were beautifully manicured Italian cypresses. They gave the garden a sense of both elegance and privacy and, best of all, they created shadow. Turner commented on them.

'They were here when we moved in, although they were a bit raggedy,' said Chris.

'They're great,' said Turner, taking a picture, 'they would make for a nice backdrop.'

Anna and Debbie emerged from the house. Anna was wearing a smart blue dress and had her hair tied into a braid. She didn't look at Turner, and he couldn't help but feel a little self-conscious. His eyes were drawn constantly towards the child, and he hid behind the lens of his camera to avoid staring.

'We haven't had a family photo taken for quite a while,' said Debbie.

Turner knew why she had said this and nodded. He had decided the best thing for all concerned was he do the job quickly and left.

There were no issues with the shoot. Anna smiled and posed and appeared to relax. Turner took a variety of photos, both digital and with film. Once it was over, Anna promptly left the setting and returned to the house.

'Maybe she's just excited about the party later,' said Turner.

Turner declined a coffee before he left and as he made his way to the hall door, he got the unsettling sense of being looked at. His head turned instinctively to the stairway and there, for the briefest instant, he saw the flicker of a child moving into the upper part of the house.

'Are you okay?' asked Debbie.

'Yes,' said Turner, 'I'll have the photos ready for you by early next week.'

The truth was, he could have them ready by the next day, but he needed distance to process what had happened.

\*

After his twin sister died, ten-year-old Joe Turner was passed around relatives for a time while his parents dealt with their grief. First, he went to his maternal grandparents in the west, but he couldn't settle, and they sent him back to Dublin after barely a week where his aunt Tilly, his father's sister, a well-meaning but flaky dreamer who smelled of patchouli and entertained strangers on nothing but a whim, took him in as a good deed to the universe. For a month, Joe sat in his high-ceilinged room day and night and listened to the constant thump of disco music and hubbub of voices. It was summertime so there was no school and during his waking hours he mostly had to fend for himself. Many a morning, he came downstairs to find Tilly passed out on the couch. Sometimes there'd be other people too. A man, who he got to know as Digby, would give him some money and tell him to go off and enjoy himself. Reflecting on this years later, Turner would say Digby was about as close as he got to having a father.

Once September drew closer with school about to resume, he left Tilly's and returned home, where his parents promptly told him he'd be going to boarding school. There was no negotiation and little by way of explanation. So, on a Sunday evening in early September, his father drove him the two hours to his new school. They barely spoke on the journey. Turner sat in the back, watching the city give way to the countryside and the lingering light give way to pale blue hues edged by dark navy. By the time they got there it was almost dark and a tall man in priest's robes took the boy into a cold grey building. The broad door closed with a hefty crash and Turner followed the man to a dormitory where he lay awake bewildered and alone until first light.

He lasted two weeks before he ran away, and then another week before he ran away for the final time. He was found sleeping in the lobby of a nearby hotel. He was fostered for a short time before returning to his parents, where he was met with silence and indifference. The only regular communication he experienced, other than the day-to-day, was his mother's seething

claim his sister's death was his fault. Over time, he came to believe this was true, even though he knew she had been sick for
years with Batten Disease and had died in a hospital. His memory of her was faint. After her diagnosis at age eight, they didn't
spend much time together. She became clumsy and slurred her
words. Her symptoms escalated aggressively, and she lost all
motor control and eventually couldn't speak. Within eighteen
months, she was removed to palliative care and within two years
of initial diagnosis, she was dead.

'Why couldn't it have been you,' were the words which became the tagline of Joe Turner's childhood.

He spent most of his teens wandering between two houses.
During school, he would live with his parents, although there
wasn't any actual living or homelife in the usual sense. His father drank a lot and his mother spent almost all her time locked
away in her bedroom. At the weekend Turner would stay with
Tilly. Tilly's carefree hedonism had been repurposed, and now
she was working in Digby's bookshop. Digby dragged Turner
through his teens by explaining to him why his parents were angry, and how he was unlucky to be caught in the crossfire. He
told Turner about his own childhood in London and about how
he'd been abandoned too. He said life often didn't make sense
and the best thing was to try not to think too much about it and
certainly not to accept any blame for things which weren't his
fault.

'Find something you love,' said Digby, 'and let it kill you.'

'What do you mean?' said Turner.

'You can figure that out for yourself. Remember, only you
have the power to define your life.'

The defining moment in Turner's life came on his fifteenth
birthday. It was a Sunday, and he'd awoken to the sound of
Tilly's voice telling him to get up and come downstairs. In the
haze of sleep, he had forgotten his birthday, after all, he rarely
got to celebrate it. He arose and ruffled his thick hair before rubbing his eyes. He dressed in the crisp spring air and went downstairs.

Digby was there, and he was holding two presents wrapped in bright silver paper, each with a delicate white bow. Turner could tell one was a book. The other was a box. He had no idea how to react. His face must have revealed this fact.

'Happy birthday, Joe,' said Digby.

Digby's voice was a comforting voice. It was low and calm and had weight. Digby's words were those of someone who understood the world and its painful complexities and contradictions.

Turner sat at the breakfast table, where Tilly put a plate of pancakes before him. He looked at them drowsily before picking up a fork. After a bit, he noticed the expectancy on both Digby and Tilly's faces.

'Go on then,' said Digby, nodding towards the presents.

Turner pulled at the bow on the box-shaped parcel, and it gave a little before twisting into a knot.

'Rip it up, mate,' said Digby cheerfully, 'have a little enthusiasm.'

Turner smiled and grabbed the parcel with both hands and ripped, as if all his frustration and anger were being released in this moment of kindness. With the paper ripped away, Turner opened the box with the same energy. Inside there was a Nikon F3 camera. He took it out and held it. It was sturdy and heavy, and there was a bit of wear and tear on the casing.

'I noticed how much you liked looking at things and now when you go on those long walks of yours you can snap things you like,' said Digby.

'That way it's forever,' added Tilly, 'I hope you like it.'

Turner looked through the viewfinder and scanned the room. The first picture he took was of a smiling Tilly and Digby. It remained with him into his adult life.

*

Turner expected to see orbs in the images from the photoshoot, but there were none. Later, when he was hanging the black and whites to dry, he noticed a double exposure in a picture of Anna. As the image dried, a smudge appeared over her shoulder. The smudge grew definition and within a few minutes there was a copy of what looked like Anna's face, but more boyish. It lay in the exact spot where an orb had appeared in the photo he'd taken of Debbie at the school. He dismissed it as another example of seeing patterns where there were none. Digital photography could create all kinds of interesting effects, but genuine, accidental double exposures were rare. Echoes of his newspaper days reverberated, as did long quiet noises from the days before his sister became ill.

'There is a good twin and a bad twin,' said their neighbour, an older girl with a sense of spite.

'The good twin always dies before the bad twin.'

The comment made his sister cry.

He called Debbie the next day and said he'd drop the pictures into the school, but she insisted he come over to the house for dinner.

'Chris would enjoy talking to an adult other than me,' said Debbie, 'he works with a bunch of loud kids, I guess we both do, and since the weekend he's dusted off his camera and been snapping everything in sight.'

Turner suppressed his first thought, preferring generosity over cynicism.

'What does he do?' he asked.

'IT. He's the only person in the company over thirty-five.'

'I see,' said Turner, giving himself time to mull over the offer.

'What about Anna?' he said, 'I'm not sure she liked me much.'

'Oh, you should pay no attention to her behaviour last weekend, she was a little out of sorts. It's got nothing to do with you.'

Turner knew it had everything to do with him.

'Birthdays are stressful for her. Anyway, she'll probably leave us alone. Usually, she has her nose stuck in a book or something like that. She's a solitary child and seems happy by herself.'

'Why are birthdays stressful for her?'

There was a pause on the other end.

'I didn't mean to pry,' said Turner.

'It's fine,' said Debbie.

Turner looked at the framed picture of Digby and Tilly. Both were smiling. Digby's voice moved on the air. Digby, who had saved him from a hard childhood and left him not long after he'd graduated from college. Digby, whose afterimage lingered behind Turner's eyes, allowing him to see through the fog. Digby, who never spurned the chance to try something new, was now telling him to go.

*Rip it up, mate, make some new friends.*

Maybe it was time to move into the unknown.

'I'll be there,' he said.

This time he was more certain about what was compelling him.

*

He took a cab on the arranged night and two bottles of wine. He struggled to remember the last time he'd been to someone's house for dinner. He thought about how he'd found her after all this time and how he would tell her. In the imagined conversation, Debbie looked at him dumbfounded by his question, and he became overwhelmed by embarrassment. He had to shut his eyes tight to make it go away.

'Are you alright there?' asked the cab driver.

Turner saw the driver's eyes in the rearview mirror.

'Yeah, just a little tired.'

Turner closed his eyes and moved his feet as they had begun to become uncomfortable. The driver looked at him again and saw Turner's closed eyes. They continued for a few minutes until

Turner asked the driver to pull over. He wanted to walk, take in the air, and prepare himself for what might come. The evening was still. A thin weave of cloud traversed the sky, and the blue-black hues of night backdropped the emerging stars. Turner searched for the familiar line of Orion's belt rising in the south-east. From there he drew a line to Aldebaran, the eye of Taurus, and from there up along the bull's horns to Castor and Pollux, the twins. He stood for a while just looking. Thoughts came and went, and for a moment Turner was fixed to the ground like a rigid and ancient cedar. He came to with the self-conscious realisation of how odd he must look standing there staring at the sky. He glanced around to see if there was anyone there and finding only the dusky emptiness, he moved on.

Chris answered the door. He was wearing the black and white stripes of a chef's apron. Turner handed him the wine a little gauchely, bumbling an excuse about not knowing if his hosts preferred red or white.

'Sure, no matter what colour, as long as it gets you drunk.'

'I suppose.'

'Won't you come in,' said Chris.

Warm aromas drifted from the kitchen. Chris hurried back to his task, while Debbie brought Turner into a drawing room and offered him a drink. He felt anxious about holding a fine balance between sociability and being sober. A few drinks would do no harm, one before dinner, one with dinner and maybe one afterward.

Dinner was good. Turner appreciated Chris' efforts. Digby had taught Turner to cook and cook well. The conversation during the meal was perfectly unremarkable, and Turner began to relax. True to Debbie's word, Anna did not bother them. This deepened Turner's calm.

Shortly after dinner, they examined the photos from the previous weekend.

'That's a good one,' he said, handing it to Debbie.

'Wow,' said Chris, leaning in.

'How do you do it?' asked Debbie.

Turner didn't reply. He enjoyed the wine's warmth and how it mingled with their words.

'These are perfect,' said Debbie, her hand coming up to cover the astonished "o" of her mouth.

A short time later, Anna stepped into the room. She curled into her father's lap like a cat and browsed the photos. Chris, realising she was tired, lifted her up and carried her to bed. In his absence, Debbie sat looking at a photo of Anna standing alone before a cypress tree.

'I think I like this one best.'

'The trees really work in that one,' said Turner, 'the light and shadow catches her face. It's as if she's two different people.'

'She had a twin brother,' said Debbie.

From the moment he had first laid eyes on her, he had known this.

'Adam, he was stillborn.'

'We tried for another a few years afterward,' said Chris, 'but Anna was all the universe gave us.'

Debbie laughed abruptly. It startled Turner.

'Sorry, that must have come across as a bit ridiculous.'

Chris came back into the room before Turner mustered his thoughts. Debbie asked Chris if Anna was okay. He nodded.

'More wine?' he said, gesturing towards the recently opened bottle on a side table.

Turner swirled the last mouthful of wine in his glass. It rolled it up the curved sides and watched as it fell back down, leaving a sheen of red and gold on the glass. He watched as tiny bubbles moved to the wine's surface before bursting and vanishing forever. He lifted the glass to his lips and threw it back.

'Please,' he said, offering his glass for a refill.

*

A week later, Turner placed an A4 envelope through Debbie and Chris' letterbox. It contained the double exposure. They had a right to find meaning in it if there was any. He understood the risk. The photo might open old wounds. They might accuse him of doctoring the photo as part of some sick joke. Then again, they may see nothing. Maybe because they never knew their child or watched him grow up, the effect would be less impactful.

The sun rose towards noon and there was heat in it. A solitary plane traversed the blue, leaving a white line of condensation in its wake. Turner watched it and thought about going somewhere, it didn't matter where as long as it was far away. He closed his eyes and let the sun's warmth soothe his face. He inhaled deeply. The subtle scents in the air reminded him of an August afternoon so many years before. He and his twin sat in long dry grass blowing dandelion clocks into the moment's bursting heart, watching the tiny umbrellas fly in skittish ascent to the gigantic sky above them.

Back then, they believed they would live forever.

# ON CORONADO BEACH

The sweeping arc of the bridge to Coronado Island is as breathtaking as it is banal. It rises through the San Diego docks like a stretching cat made sluggish by the California sun. The ascent is gradual, so you don't notice the height until you begin to imagine what would happen if there was an accident and then every bit of its two hundred feet grabs at you like a frightened child, if such things bother you. They don't bother me. I don't mind being high up, whether it's on a bridge going sixty or a plane going six hundred, it makes no odds how far above ground you are, it's a way of getting places. The rise doesn't last, you are beginning to descend before you realise it, and that's when the island comes into view. It's not much to look at, but in a car with the top open on a July day, it's better than being dead. The bridge is America's second favourite suicide bridge, though I can't understand why you'd want to kill yourself if you lived in San Diego, aside from the fact *Top Gun* was filmed there. Yeah, when it comes to leaving this life it's second only to the Golden Gate Bridge and there I was thinking the Golden State was full of happy golden people, goes to show, doesn't it?

This was the first time we crossed the bridge together. Susan, my wife, had been to San Diego years before and in her excited giddiness she made the crossing to the island sound exhilarating and wonderful. But like everything fuelled by anticipation, nostalgia and imagination, it fell short. Mustering my best acting, I told her it was amazing and how I was having a great time. I asked our ten-year-old son, who was sitting in the backseat, if he was having a good time, but he was too busy chasing images on a screen. It occurred to me how his generation was likely to be underwhelmed by everything because reality would never catch up with the fizzing neurons of their gamer existence.

We sloped down the final stretch of the bridge and on to the island. An old tollbooth, its canopy still intact, sat squat and sun-bleached like something left behind on the set of a sci-fi film. I made a quip about free entry to the island, but no one commented.

We parked somewhere off Avenue B or C. In the warmth of the day it didn't matter, we had no particular place to go and plenty of time to get there. I asked Susan about it, but she said nothing and strolled ahead with the boy, now gadget free and enjoying the heat. My thoughts wandered in the lazy warmth, and I found myself appreciating the manicured lawns, the tidy streets and the flags hanging from flagpoles like landed marlins. As I ambled along, I saw an old man, perhaps eighty, maybe more, trudge one step at a time up a small path and then move stiffly up the wooden steps to his porch before finally flopping into a wicker chair like someone who'd been holding a secret and now suddenly unburdened could relax. His sense of relief for having made it to safety made me think about the peculiarly American sense of pride in one's home, and why Americans felt so strongly about their guns and their right to bear them. I looked back at the old man and imagined him levelling a rifle at me and winking and telling me to keep on walking and leave him be.

A loud and powerful pickup truck chugged past, leaving the smell of petrol and gears and mechanical processes in its wake. It unmoored me from my daydreaming, and I looked at Susan, who was about fifty feet ahead and nearing the end of the street. She was pointing to the right, indicating the direction in which I was to follow her. She turned the corner and I jogged to catch up. By the time I got to the corner, she was, once again, fifty feet ahead.

After another short street and a couple of more turns, we arrived on Orange Street where Susan became animated as if privy to some delicious gossip. She smiled broadly and said she knew where she was and how it was all coming back to her. She skipped ahead with the boy and in the wind after her, I caught her words, faint and delicate like a dragonfly's wings, the hotel, the beach, *Some Like it Hot.*

The hotel was like any other. Opulent and grand, for sure, with an airport concourse-like reception and gift shops and teeming tourists flashing along corridors. I knew the reason for its fame and while I liked the movie, I wasn't especially impressed. While my wife and son walked through the cool foyer and out towards the courtyard leading to the beach, I paused to ask a bellhop how much a room cost per night and once I'd had a moment to process the information I followed on. The courtyard led to a set of double doors through which, red-carpeted stairs dropped into a small garden and from there to the dry white heat of the beach.

They were waiting on the stairs and once I arrived, they moved on. *Race you,* said the boy, his mother following in gleeful chase. I watched them go towards the white sand and stop abruptly, as if it had turned to shards of glass.

*You are missing it,* Susan said, urging me to hurry up. I thought to myself I was missing nothing, that whatever was there would still be there when I arrived. I ambled along and when I got there, I asked what it was I was missing. Susan gave me a distant look and then told me matter-of-factly that the sand was too hot to walk on barefoot. It was.

We took a spot near enough to the water for the boy to play unsupervised. He gravitated to the rocks and rock pools and after enduring some small talk with my wife, I left her to the sun and followed the boy. He was among a group of blonde-haired kids who may or may not have been related. His dark hair made him recognisable to me, as I'd forgotten the colour of his t-shirt. Approaching him, I noticed it was red, white and blue, of course.

The assembly of kids were looking at crabs scuttling under the rocks and across the rocks or standing absolutely still, waving their pincers in a touchingly feeble display of threat. *Get them, get that one*, said a kid who was reaching for a bucket and plunging it into the water of a deeper pool. Once full, a hand deposited a crab into it, then another crab until there were several crabs circling the bottom of the bucket. The boy and I peered in. I said something to him, half expecting someone to say *you're not from 'round here to me*, but nothing was said and the boy who was now welcome in the group moved on to the larger rocks spreading into the ocean in a ragged path.

At that moment, I had the astounding primal realisation I was standing in the Pacific. I looked at how it stretched into a pile of grey and white cloud, and how much darker the water appeared than what movies would have you believe.

I said those exact words to a woman who appeared to my right. I don't know why I said it, maybe I thought it needed to be said.

'Are you from England?' she asked.

'Ireland,' I said.

'My husband always wanted to go there.'

I didn't reply, but my natural cynicism about the American cliché of visiting Ireland began to rise. I expected her to compliment my brogue or tell me about her relatives in some godforsaken part of West Cork. I let words come to the surface but passed on the chance to commentate and instead took a surreptitious look at the woman by pretending to focus on an imaginary point down the beach.

She was older than me, mid-fifties perhaps, I couldn't tell exactly, but I could tell she'd miles on the clock. Despite this, she retained something of youthful attractiveness. Her hair was blonde, and she was slim. I pictured her as a younger woman on the beaches of La Jolla or Newport in the company of some surfer, discussing a future which had since come to pass.

'He never got there,' she said.

'There's still time,' I said offhandedly.

'He died two weeks ago.'

'I'm sorry,' I said automatically, and then thought how hollow it sounded.

'How do you like it here, in California?'

It was then I noticed her accent, it was broader and slower than a generic American accent, as if every word had to earn its place, and for an instant, I thought of *Fargo*. I asked her where she was from.

'I live in Phoenix,' she said, 'but I come from a small town in Maine.'

'Aren't all towns in Maine small?'

She smiled and, as a small wind rose, pulled her hair away from her face.

'I guess so,' she said, 'same as Ireland.'

I nodded in appreciation of her riposte.

'Was your husband from Maine?'

'New York,' she said.

'How long have you lived in Phoenix?'

'About a week.'

I didn't know what to say. I looked at the rocks to where the boy, now fully integrated into the blonde clique, was climbing with the casual steadiness of a cat. I looked again at the woman and then behind me to where Susan lay on the sand, the whiteness of her skin making her almost invisible.

'A new beginning,' said the woman, 'just in case you're wondering about why I moved to Phoenix.'

I didn't comment. I smiled in a way which I hoped conveyed a willingness to listen. I felt she had more to say.

'We lived in New York for almost thirty years. He was a stockbroker, he worked non-stop, chasing all the money in the world. In the end, he smoked, drank and stressed himself to death.'

She paused before continuing. Her voice carried an echo of wistfulness, but it was faint and dwindled like a dying ember with each word.

'We had three kids, and we never travelled anywhere or did anything. He was all about work and golf. I looked after the kids and when they moved on, I'd nothing to do anymore.'

I was about to parrot another sorry when a cry of delight rang out from the ocean, startling me. I saw a girl rising from the water on the shoulders of a muscular young man. He took hold of her waist and threw her into the air. It was like something you'd see on the beaches of Magaluf or Ayia Napa, young people enjoying themselves in the sunrise of their lives. I watched as she hung in the air and for a moment everything stopped before she crashed into the water with a loud splash.

'Aside from the fresh start, why Phoenix, why not Maine?' I asked.

The woman didn't seem to object to the question but took a moment to reply.

'The weather.'

'My wife's the same.'

'My husband didn't care for the sun. He was a cold person, in every sense of the word.'

I wanted to ask her if she was glad he was gone, for my own satisfaction, but I didn't need to, the tiny trace of a smile on her face was like a flower emerging in spring, unaccustomed to its new surroundings, only needing time to bloom.

'You be good to your wife,' she said to me, 'treat her right.'

'How do you know I don't?' I asked.

It was her turn to look beyond me and into the distance.

I wanted to press the point, but I knew it would be better if I didn't say anything.

The boy came running towards me, his face filled with energy and urgency. He told me in a breathless gasp he'd seen a huge crab and I had to come and look at it.

*It's ginormous,* he said, his eyes wide as saucers.

I told him I'd be over in a minute, and he ran off with the same urgency as he'd arrived.

'He's a good-looking boy,' said the woman.

'Thanks.'

'You'd better go see the crab before it scuttles away,' she said in a voice which conveyed a sense of purpose.

I nodded. She was right. I began to make my move.

'I threw his ashes in the water just beyond those rocks,' she said, almost as an afterthought.

I looked at the rocks and how the waves threw up a white and frothy spray onto them.

'It's a beautiful place,' I said, 'seems as good a place as any to do something like that.'

'He hated the beach,' she said.

I turned to look at her, but she'd turned and was moving with casual ease up the shoreline. The waves crashed and broke and stretched along the sand and almost tickled her feet, but not quite. My eyes trailed up the sand to where Susan was waving at me. She was pointing at the boy.

He called to me again, and I began to run towards him, hoping all the time the crab would still be there when I arrived.

# WHEN INSECTS WERE AS BIG AS BIRDS

I was in work when my brother called to tell me Willo Hicks was dead. It was a cold Tuesday in early March. In the moment's overwhelming suddenness, I thought of the joke.

*What did Willo Hicks die of?*

*He died of a Tuesday.*

'Ray, are you there?' said my brother.

'Yeah, sorry, I zoned out for a moment.'

'I did the same when I heard.'

A pause followed, like the space between scenes of a movie. Finally, my brother spoke.

'No details yet about a funeral or anything. I'll keep you posted.'

I thanked him and hung up.

I'd known Willo since we were little kids but, in our twenties, we'd lost touch. Then, out of the blue, about three months before his death, he'd sent me a message suggesting we meet up. I replied, saying it was a good idea, but for one reason or another, it never happened. My brother and a few lads met up with him in late January. He later admonished me for not going.

'I have kids, life is busy, I can't just drop things like you.'

'Suit yourself, anyway, he was asking for you.'

'I'll try and catch up with him soon.'

'You should,' said my brother, before adding, 'he seems to be in a good place.'

'Yeah?'

'He's more stable than when I last saw him.'

Willo Hicks struggled his whole life. He was smart as a whip and schoolwork came easy to him, but like many smart kids, he got bored and lost interest in almost everything except drawing. We'd be in English class and Mr. Barton, who we nicknamed 'Mr. Boreton', would be droning on about Shakespeare or one of those old writers who made studying literature miserable.

Willo, who gave the impression he was miles away, would be listening, but he'd also be doodling, and Barton would prowl around him before pouncing and snatching whatever Willo was drawing. It was usually amazing, sometimes it was pure imagination. Sometimes it was related to the lesson. During our reading of *Hamlet*, Willo did a pencil drawing. The Dane was looking out a huge window in Elsinore. The drawing had the intricate, ornate detail of a medieval church. I couldn't fathom how a mind could imagine such a scene, let alone bring it to life on a blank page. Willo's Hamlet looked lost in thought, as if he were trying to make sense of something which couldn't be articulated.

Under the drawing, Willo had written:

*I could be bounded in a nutshell and count myself a king of infinite space, were it not that I have bad dreams.*

Barton held it up to the class, but on this occasion, he refrained from making a derogatory comment. He passed it around and told us to study the drawing. He then retrieved it and praised Willo.

'Normally,' he said in his typically sardonic tone, 'I wouldn't condone artwork during English class, but this is very nice indeed. Isn't it lads?' Later in the year, the drawing became the school's literary magazine cover. The thing was, though, it didn't give Willo any satisfaction to see this. I think he felt his art had been misappropriated and, much like Hamlet, he retreated into himself. I couldn't explain why. A lot of Willo's behaviour was beyond explanation.

He began drinking around that time. It wasn't until much later I understood the cause and content of Willo's bad dreams.

He became a regular drinker. We were no different from any other teens. We drank to get drunk and liked a party. Willo would often start slow, but after a few beers he'd become animated, and then he'd hit the hard stuff, usually vodka. My tolerance for it was poor, and I would often end up outside in the garden puking on the roses or once in a raised bed of lettuce. Anyway, with a few drinks in him, Willo would get high on life and this in turn would intoxicate those around him. Sometimes it was pure fun, sometimes it was surreal.

'What would be the worst way to die?' he said to those who'd gathered at his court. It was two in the morning at Anna McGuire's house, and the party was beginning to dwindle. The assembled, mostly lads, had no clue what to say.

'Quint,' he slurred, 'in *Jaws*. That was brutal. Eaten alive by a huge fucking shark.'

'Someone suggested the face melting in *Raiders of the Lost Ark*.

'Riding your ma,' said someone, causing the whole place to collapse into laughter.

'I propose a committee to investigate the worst way to die,' said Willo once the laughter subsided. He then jumped imperiously on a chair, held his balance for a superb moment before losing it and pitching headlong and unceremoniously on top of a quiet, and startled pixie-type girl who was dozing on the couch. She awoke with a scream, rattling everyone into a kind of feral alertness.

This girl, Lisa, became his girlfriend, then his wife and then his ex-wife.

At his funeral, she asked me if I'd be a pallbearer.

'You were like a brother to him, all of you were like brothers.'

I said I'd be honoured and then felt the fierce sting of cold steel in my chest for being a fraud, for not meeting up with him when I had the chance.

Willo's father approached us as we gathered to lift the coffin.

'It's a hard blow,' he said, 'but you boys being here helps. Thank you.'

We carried the coffin to the hearse, and I swear it weighed a million tonnes. As we lifted it down, I felt my left leg buckle and for a second, I imagined the worst. Steo Palmer laughed out loud.

'Steady on there, Rayo, this is not a time for butterfingers.'

At the crematorium, Willo's father spoke in the way only a parent who's burying their child can. He related the story of how Willo, whose real name was Patrick, got his nickname.

'He was a mind of information,' said Willo's father, 'but sure you all know that.'

He paused and then spoke about the time when Willo was thirteen. He'd recently discovered cricket and told everyone he met how cricket bats were made from the wood of willow trees, and how the Latin name for willow was Salix.

'He'd drive you demented with the stuff he knew,' continued Willo's father, 'sometimes my head would be spinning so fast with information, I'd have to lie down after listening to him.'

He continued in this manner before reciting a poem he'd written for the occasion. There wasn't a dry eye in the place. A hard lump caught thickly in my throat and lingered there for days after. Finally, the coffin disappeared behind a curtain, and so it was for Willo Hicks' earthly remains.

After the cremation, we gathered at The Cedar House, Willo's local. When he'd separated from Lisa, he'd moved back home and every Friday night, without fail, you'd find Willo and his father having a few pints and setting the world to right. Sometimes they'd insist you sit with them, other times they were deep in the weeds of some philosophical discussion and wild horses couldn't distract them.

Standing in the pub, looking at the tables Willo used to occupy, I didn't feel right. The whole thing felt off. Everyone was having a drink and a chat, but I couldn't loosen up.

'Nearly caused a scene there with the coffin.'

A hand clasped my shoulder in the forceful but friendly way some men are. It was Steo Palmer. A few seconds later, my brother and the other lads joined us. Steo continued ribbing me and I tried to smile and join in, but I wasn't in the mood for banter. I sipped my drink and then on the pretext of going to the toilet I slipped out the door and stood in the street.

The growing shroud of night began to fall. It was cold, but I enjoyed its bracing touch. *It should have been me*, I kept thinking, *it should have been me*. Since Willo's death, I'd been turning one event over and over in my mind. I'd tried for years to dismiss it, but the night when we determined which of us would die first resurfaced with a vengeance when I'd learned of Willo's death and I could no longer ignore it, even if I knew correlation and causation were not the same thing.

Sometimes, after the lights and drink at a party had flickered out, Willo and I would end up walking home together. This was usually on account of having no money for a cab, but sometimes it was to have a chat. The walk could be as short as a few streets or much, much longer. One June morning, at about two, Willo and I left a party in Sutton and began the long walk home. The sky was rich indigo with a big milky moon. The familiar summer constellations hung on it like glittering pins on a curtain. To our left, the sea spread into the bay. The moonlight rippled over the water like a silver ribbon. We were about to walk along the seaside road when Willo turned to look at me. He was drunk, but there was a mellowness to his mood, and his eyes sparkled with an idea.

'Let's walk along the train tracks,' he said excitedly.

I began to reply, but he grabbed my arm and manoeuvred me towards the tracks.

'Don't worry, there are no trains at this hour.'

A few minutes later we were climbing over the barrier to the tracks and after a minute we were standing on the platform. Willo slowly and theatrically looked first one way and then the other.

'See,' he said, no trains.'

35

We began to walk. I stumbled on the sleepers a couple of times. More than once, I almost fell headfirst onto them, but each time Willo caught me.

'You are the clumsiest fucker, Rayo. I swear it'll be the death of you.'

'Probably,' I agreed.

We sang *Hotel California* and *Layla* to pass the time, but mostly we talked.

*

Willo was everyone's friend, but circumspect about who he confided in. I was one of those people. I won't bore you with the details, as most were the mundane anxieties of being a young adult in a world which saw you as an outsider while expecting you to fit in. Yes, Willo and I were a bit awkward and a bit depressed and a bit lots of other things. Invariably, our conversations turned to death. These weren't the whimsical musings about the worst way to die, no, these were speculations about death.

We spoke about everything, but mostly about the afterlife and what it might be. Willo's pet theory was each of us lived several lives, some good, some bad. Afterward, we moved on to whatever came next. He surmised a life free from suffering wasn't a real life. If it was easy, as far as he was concerned, it wasn't worthwhile.

We were in the middle of one of these conversations when a high-pitched noise like the squeak of air being let out of a balloon began to resonate up and down the tracks.

'A train,' I said.

There was no real danger. We were in an unlit section, but we weren't in a tunnel or on a bridge. There was room for us to climb safely up the steep bank. Unexpectedly, the train's impending approach began to excite me. Willo was smiling, and his eyes shone with a familiar light. He stood in the middle of the tracks.

'I'm going to wait for it and dodge it.'

'Don't be stupid.'

In the distance, the pale-yellow glow of a moving light began to emerge from the dark.

'Seriously,' I said, 'let's climb up the bank and wait for it to pass.'

'Boring,' said Willo, in an exaggerated manner, 'you can do that, I'm waiting here.'

I couldn't win. Willo was as intractable as a dog with a bone. I retreated to the bank and watched as Willo stood in a defiant crouch.

There was no way of telling how near the train was. The light was pale like an underwater shimmer, and in the semi-darkness our depth perception was poor. The only way we could tell was the gathering noise. As it grew, I retreated further up the bank, all evidence of earlier excitement now replaced by concern for my friend. What happened next is a surreal portrait in my memory. I can't be certain it happened in the way I describe it here, but whenever I recall it, it's always the same.

The train's chugging rattle was now thunderous. Its light was beginning to fill the available space, and the bank became much smaller. I tried to move further up the bank when I slipped and slid dramatically down the incline. I clawed at the loose stones crumbling beneath me and slid downwards, unable to get purchase.

All at once, the noise from the train became deafening. It was barrelling down on me like some ancient monster, and I was sliding helplessly towards it. I cried out, but in the noise, I had no idea if any sound came from my mouth or just a feeble croak. The train couldn't have been more than a hundred feet away when my shoes hit the track's edge. I could feel its pulsing force bounce through me, and all I could think of was why I couldn't stop myself from falling towards it. The train passed by with a whooshing primal roar and I felt the wind under the edge of its clearance brush within inches of my toes. I lay there, pinned to the earth, and waited for it to rip my feet from me and suck me into its mechanical processes and chew me up.

When it began to recede into the darkness, I continued laying there, my chest heaving and my heart racing. I stayed there for some time until I opened my eyes and saw the shape of Willo leaning over me.

'That was cool,' he said in his best Butthead impression.

'What?'

'I saw the whole thing; you almost fell down the bank.'

'What?'

'Forget it, get up.'

'Can we go home a different way?' I asked.

Willo lifted me up and, with wobbly legs, we walked the short distance to where we could climb a railing and get off the tracks.

'You dodged it.'

I didn't reply, I knew where his thoughts were going.

'You could have easily fallen onto the tracks or been sucked under the train, but you weren't, it wasn't your time.'

'Can we sing something and go home? I'm not in the mood for this now.'

'Okay, Rayo,' said Willo, 'but tell you what, I bet you anything I'm going to go before you.'

I shook my head.

'No,' he said animatedly, 'listen to me, it makes sense, it skipped you and moved to me. You were meant to fall down the bank and get smushed, but you weren't, fate, man. Destiny.'

'That's ridiculous,' I said.

'No,' said Willo, 'in the Precambrian Era, insects were as big as birds. Now that's ridiculous. Imagine a wasp the size of a swan.'

I laughed out loud and almost immediately the laughter turned to tears, a waterfall of them. Willo embraced me, and we stood there while I cried it out.

Willo's house was the first stop. It was almost four and the first hints of dawn were emerging from the night in thin rosy wisps.

'Don't forget this,' said Willo, 'you've got a lot of life to live, Rayo.'

I nodded, and he smiled and turned down the driveway and within a few seconds, he was gone.

Lisa's voice broke my reverie.

It took me a moment to acknowledge her. I asked her if Willo had told her about the train.

'Yes,' she said, 'and how you cried.'

I felt my cheeks flush.

'He loved you, Ray, he loved all of you, but you were the one he loved most.'

'I didn't see him when I had the chance.'

'I know,' said Lisa, 'but maybe it was for the best, he wasn't the same guy you knew.'

'My brother met him, he said he was doing well.'

Lisa looked at the ground.

'Are you coming back inside?'

'No, I think I'll head home.'

She leaned in and kissed me softly on the cheek.

'Thanks for everything today, Ray.'

She went back inside, and I pulled my coat around me and walked towards home.

On the way, I took a detour. I stood on a bridge overlooking the same tracks Willo and I walked all those years before. I leaned over and followed the twin lines into the dark as far as I could with my eyes. I did this for a while and was completely absorbed in it when I heard the distant rumble of an approaching train. I decided to wait. I knew it was close and getting closer. Before long, the air coming from under the bridge became restless and smelled different. The bridge began to shake and within seconds the train raged along the tracks with the fury of a dragon.

As it passed, I resisted the strange urge welling up inside me. Instead, I shouted into the deafening noise until my lungs were empty and my throat hurt. After it had gone, I sank onto the ground and peered into the dark sky until my mind became quiet, and I could finally get up and go home.

# THE GHOSTS OF DEVIL'S DEN

A squat grey building of only thirty-four stories. The sky exhaled its grey breath, so the building merged with the persistent gloom filling the peripheries of my vision, making me feel as if I were enclosed in a particularly melancholic impressionist painting.

My gut told me to turn around and go back to New York, but my greed pulled me towards the building. I'd never felt hesitancy like this before, and I was not going to let it get the better of me.

It was early March and bitter cold, and I couldn't figure out why a man of his wealth would run his business empire from such an ugly and unimpressive place. The building lacked all distinction and class one might associate with wealth and power. It jutted out of the city's otherwise elegant skyline, looming like an oversized tooth.

I stood before its solid facade with more questions beginning to form in my mind. I dismissed them with the dispassionate efficiency of a farmer drowning kittens. In my line of work, curiosity was an unnecessary distraction. I took a deep breath through my nose and made my way up the broad granite steps to the main door, where after a moment, a humourless man greeted me by asking my name.

'Ford,' I said. 'I'm here to see Mr. Walker.'

'This way, please,' said the man.

We rode the elevator in the type of silence only those accustomed to serving the extremely wealthy knew. There was no point trying to engage this man in small talk, he would ignore me and continue staring implacably ahead. After what seemed longer than it was, we climbed to the seventeenth floor.

The elevator stopped and then sank into its resting position. The man stood aside and told me to go to Room 179, which, he said, was just down the hall to the left. Once there, I was to knock once upon the door.

'Knock once, Mr. Ford, and only once. Mr. Walker doesn't care for people who cannot follow simple instructions.'

The man's voice had the calculating authority of a trial judge. I nodded and exited the elevator. As I walked down the corridor, I felt the walls close in on me, the hallway becoming narrower and narrower. I stopped and tried to compose myself, but a powerful feeling of isolation struck. It was as if I'd travelled in time to a desolate future or barren past. I took a deep breath and after a few seconds the feeling of unease lifted. Finding myself in front of Walker's office door, I reached up to knock; the sense of un-ease returned briefly like a cold wind, making me hesitate. *What is wrong with you*? I curled my fingers into my palm and rapped once on the door. I heard the shuffle of feet. The door opened and Mr. Walker invited me in.

He was tall with an angular face. His facial hair reminded me of men from bygone eras. His complexion matched the day's pallor, and I reasoned he spent much of his time indoors. He was dressed smartly in a dark suit; I could see the gold chain of a pocket watch from inside the silk folds of his jacket.

He pointed to a plush chair in front of an imposing mahogany desk. I sank into it, struggling momentarily as the chair failed to support my weight. I awkwardly manoeuvred my body so I could sit up straight. Walker observed my brawl with the chair with interest, and I noticed a wry smile flickering at the edge of his mouth. Once I had control of the situation, it vanished, and Walker's expression became firm and unreadable.

'Did you have a pleasant journey, Mr. Ford?'

I'd flown from New York that morning, there had been strong crosswinds during take-off and landing. At least once during take-off and twice during landing I had feared for my safety and though I don't believe in God or such things, I intoned a silent prayer of thanks once we were on the ground.

'It was fine,' I said, perfunctorily.

Walker's desk was spare and functional. There was a telephone, two pens in an upright stand, a photo frame whose subject I could not see and a bronze statuette of what I suspected was a Union cavalryman. My eyes must have lingered on it for longer than usual, and Walker seized upon the moment.

'Do you like it?' he said in a cordial, even warm voice which invited a response.

This bonhomie threw me a little. Walker stood up and pushed the statuette towards me. Mindful of my precarious balance, I reached forward gingerly, picked it up, and examined it the way I might inspect something before buying it. It was heavier than I expected, and its marble base felt colder than it ought to be.

'Very nice,' I said, returning it to the desk.

'That is Brigadier General John Henry Hobart Ward.'

My expression must have conveyed a lack of interest, as the previous friendliness in Walker's voice developed an edge. Not only was there a palpable perception of underlying hostility bubbling to the surface, but there was something about the manner of his words I couldn't place. They were slow and deliberate and out of place in the modern world.

'You're not familiar with Civil War history, are you, Mr. Ford?' said Walker directly.

'No,' I said. 'I haven't looked at a history book since high school.' 'A man who doesn't know history is a man adrift in the world.' Walker's eyes met mine and remained there. I held the stare long enough to get a measure of the man and let him measure me. I was used to dealing with powerful types and was not intimidated. In the years of fulfilling the various tasks I'd been assigned by them, I had become accustomed to how they worked. They were all the same. They wanted you to acknowledge their superiority.

'Is a familiarity with history relevant to the task, Mr. Walker?' I asked. 'It's not essential,' said Walker, 'but some education of the history of this great nation would be no harm, even if only for your own personal edification, Mr. Ford.'

I bristled slightly at the word *harm*. There was no weight in how Walker expressed the word, but the earlier feeling of isolation returned. He pointed to the statuette.

'A great man,' he said in a tone that was almost wistful. 'General Ward was a great patriot, but you won't find his name in many history books, and if you do, it'll be nothing more than a footnote.'

After a moment in which he appeared to be savouring his words, Walker proceeded to tell me about how Ward, with relatively few men and no reserves, held the ground between the Wheatfield Road and Devil's Den at Gettysburg. The story was somewhat entertaining, and he spoke enthusiastically. I tried to look interested and must have appeared engaged, for Walker grew as he told the tale in the way a storyteller with the right audience does.

'They say Plum Run ran red with the blood of the dead for days.' I nodded.

'Are you a superstitious man, Mr. Ford?'

'No.'

'A man in your line of work hasn't got the luxury of being superstitious, I suppose,' said Walker offhandedly as if he were thinking out loud. I didn't elaborate, there was nothing to add; Walker had made his mind up, and I was not going to submit to his shake down. His eyes returned to fix their gaze on me. I waited for him to speak.

Another thing I'd learned about powerful men, they appreciated it when you listened.

'You see, many people say Devil's Den is haunted, cursed even. I reckon a place that has seen so much bloodshed must be. Don't you reckon too, Mr. Ford?'

'My grandfather told stories about the Civil War when I was a kid,' I said. 'I think he tried to throw a scare into us.'

'Your family is from the Boston area, Mr. Ford?' Walker's tone had the sombre quality of a prosecutor.

I'd expected this. Walker had a reputation for meticulous research. It was no secret I hailed from Boston, but the way he was specific about my family had the effect of a cold scalpel cutting through flesh.

'Yes, Somerville,' I said. My focus was on remaining calm. 'My family is from New York, but I no longer care for the city. I find it too raucous for my tastes. I prefer the countryside's quietude. I like to sit outside in the summer months and watch hummingbirds come to the feeder. Nature is such a boon to man. Do you contemplate the natural world, Mr. Ford?'

'Not especially.'

'While hummingbirds and butterflies and such things are pretty,' said Walker, 'the thing I enjoy most is seeing a hawk swoop down from the treetops and take up a chipmunk or rabbit in its talons. I am endlessly impressed by the brute beauty of life.'

Walker looked away, as if his eyes had caught sight of something in the distance. A look of stillness descended upon him. He remained this way for a few seconds before reaching into a desk drawer. He took out a leather-bound case, opened it, and placed a wrinkled piece of brown paper about the size of a placemat onto the desk. He pushed it toward me with his index finger, and without saying anything invited me to look at it. I leaned into the desk, and my eyes moved over the markings on the paper. It was a map. A map of the Devil's Den and environs.

'It is rumoured,' began Walker, 'a few years or so after the battle, Ward buried the gold he had plundered during the war at Devil's Den. Perhaps he believed the ghosts would protect it, or perhaps he felt a sense of conscience for profiteering. Whatever his reasons were, Mr. Ford, the fact of our small matter here is that I have recently acquired this map, and I would like you to see if there is any truth to the rumour.'

'You want me to find buried treasure?' I said in a jaundiced voice. 'I know it differs from your usual line of work,' said Walker, 'but with the right price, a man can be persuaded to do almost anything.'

I enjoyed the irony. My work mostly involved burying things, be they secrets or bodies. 'How much?' I said.

'You don't beat around the bush, do you, Mr. Ford?' said Walker with a chuckle.

'I don't see any reason for it. How much?'

'Fifty percent of any gold you find.'

I laughed aloud at the absurdly high commission and wondered at his motives.

'What if I find nothing?'

'I will cover your expenses and pay you double your daily rate for time incurred.'

I didn't much care for the thought of poking around rural Pennsylvania on what was probably a fool's errand, but if all it involved was a little bit of digging, it was easy money.

'I'll give it two days.'

'You'll probably only need one. Though it'd be best to do any excavation under cover of darkness. There will be visitors during the day, and you'd likely be prosecuted for defacing a national monument.'

'I'll be discrete.'

'I have complete faith in your attention to detail, Mr. Ford.' Walker's geniality returned. He stood up and moved to my side of the desk. He leaned over the desk and motioned for me to stand and examine the map with him, as if we were field marshals planning an attack. He looked over the map, pointing out various landmarks and where the treasure would be. He said the experts he had hired to decipher the map had narrowed it down to an area of about five square meters. I suggested that was still a considerable area to cover. He ignored my comment, and once he was satisfied I understood his instructions, he offered me his hand and I shook it. He then motioned me towards the door.

'Why me?' I asked on the way out.

The question had been burning in my mind since Walker had first made his proposition. He could have paid anyone to do this job. He could have hired a team of professional diggers and bribed someone in the Parks Department to look the other way while they chewed up the ground.

'Because you have a reputation for getting things done, and, as you mentioned already, discretion. I want this to be *sub rosa*, known only to you and me. I have a reputation to maintain and would not care for gossip, especially if our little treasure hunt proves to be a fruitless undertaking.'

I nodded in appreciation of the sentiment, but couldn't reconcile the scenario in my mind. The whole thing had a theatrical eccentricity to it. In my preparation for meeting with this man, I learned that whatever people said about Walker, a sense of whimsy was not one of his qualities.

'Mr. Winesap, whom you met earlier, will drive you to the airport. He will also issue you with a check for two thousand dollars for your time today.' I nodded and left.

\*

The next day, after a restless night in a good hotel in Harrisburg, I drove the short distance to Gettysburg. I followed Walker's directions and soon found myself at Devil's Den. There were about a dozen tourists sauntering around like cattle, but as it was getting dark, I knew they'd leave shortly.

I'd parked a short distance away from the visitor car park, confident I could evade detection by any rangers doing their rounds. It was now a waiting game, and I had the patience of a spider. I had imagined I'd be roaming a grassy field with hillocks and fences and was surprised to see something entirely different. Walker was right, I should have paid more attention to history.

The place was dominated by imposing boulders, which reminded me of the building where I'd met with Walker. They were vast, imposing rocks and looked as if they'd fallen from the sky, dropped by some careless giant from another time. There was an unsettling strangeness to them and their incongruity with the rest of the landscape.

A stiff breeze whistled through the rocks. In the wind, I thought I heard cries of the Union and Confederate dead echoing through time. The prevailing sense of isolation I'd experienced the day before reclaimed a place in my soul and despite my rational and unflappable personality, I sensed something frightening and otherworldly.

The sun was flaring in the sky, casting a dandelion sparkle over the shimmering grasses. I moved through the corridors and crannies of boulders. They were filled with a mesmerising golden light and deep, impenetrable shadows. I thought of what Walker had told me about the battle, how Confederate sharpshooters covered by the rocks had picked off Union soldiers on Little Round Top to the northeast. The wind screeched through the natural hollows and cut at me like glass.

A rising feeling of claustrophobia threatened to seize me, and I had to take deep breaths before emerging from the rocks to the grassy scrub at the foot of Little Round Top. I took out the map and looked for the two markers Walker's experts had highlighted. They were easy to find, and within a matter of minutes I was standing at the X mark on the map.

I looked around. I was alone in the quickly gathering dusk. The shadows had pushed out much of the light from the boulders in Devil's Den, and for a brief, chilling instant I thought I saw something moving slowly with the focused purpose of a predator. I shook my head and instinctively touched my gun. I planted my marker and stole away to where my car was parked about a mile distant.

By the time I returned, it was near total darkness and almost nothing was familiar. No earlier topography was discernible. I thought I'd be able to see Little Round Top rising from the land, but it was too dark. Somewhere in the depths of my mind, I had anticipated that without due diligence I'd be stumbling blindly.

Instead of trying the impossible, I'd had the foresight to use an electronic locator as a marker. I now followed its soft pulse on my phone. The wind flailed more sharply than earlier, and the imaginary cries I'd perceived within it were even louder than before. The undulating ground beneath my feet gave me the unsteady impression of being on a boat. Between the wind-harrowed night and the rolling land, the journey took much longer than my previous reconnoitre.

I stumbled twice, the second time my shin hit the hard, cold solidity of a rock. I let out a yell and had to wait for the piercing pain to subside before carrying on. My spade felt heavy on my shoulder, and when I stumbled a third time, it jarred into the ground and caught me painfully in the chest. I lay on the ground gasping. This time it took me longer to compose myself before carrying on.

At the marker, my shin still aching, I dropped my flashlight to the ground where it threw a thin yellow light into the thick darkness. I pushed the spade into the earth. It made a scratching rasp as it met the dirt. I leaned on it with my instep. My shin protested loudly, but I leaned harder, and the ground yielded. I began to dig.

After twenty minutes of determined work, I struck something solid. I knelt and began to feel my way around the edges of what I believed was a box of some kind. The giddy feeling of anticipation began to rise in my stomach. I had doubted Walker's claim, but here was proof of something buried.

I dug eagerly around the edges and soon realized to my dismay the box was longer than I had initially thought. I'd need to extend the hole along the chest's edges, and that meant more toil. I cursed into the howling wind and resumed my task. Half an hour later, I had dug out enough ground to expose all the edges and open the container.

The wind had softened but continued to lick around the darkness with a low howl followed by rasping gusts. I felt anger towards my fear but pressed on. The box was maybe four feet long, and as I tried to pry its edges, I found it stuck fast. I grabbed the flashlight and looked at it more closely. It was nailed shut, and for the first time I understood it wasn't a box filled with gold. It was a coffin and had been buried there relatively recently. It certainly wasn't a relic from the Civil War. I recoiled and scrambled to my feet. It was then I heard the familiar click of a revolver being readied to fire.

'Don't turn around, Mr. Ford.'

'Walker,' I said, 'what are you doing?'

'I don't think you're in a position to ask questions, Mr. Ford.'

I turned my head involuntarily.

'I told you not to turn around.'

'If you're going to kill me,' I said, 'I should get an explanation. I mean, it would be the civil thing to do.'

'You're right.'

I waited for him to speak; I had no idea what to do. A part of me expected to hear the burst of a gunshot before oblivion, while another part expected Walker to speak. The silence probably lasted a matter of seconds, but it felt like an eternity.

'I'm repaying an old debt,' said Walker in his slow, deliberate voice.

I thought about the hits I'd done and couldn't connect Walker to any of them.

'I don't understand.'

'I asked you back in my office if you knew any Civil War history. If you recall, I said it was a pity you didn't.'

'You said it would do me no harm.'

My heart was beating so hard I could hear blood pounding through my ears.

'You see,' continued Walker, 'the map was a ruse to get you here. There's no gold, the box is empty, but it won't be for long.'

'What did I do?' I shouted into the wind and the dark and the isolation.

'*You* did nothing, Mr. Ford. But during the battle at Devil's Den your great-great-great grandfather—one Hyram Ford, a private in Ward's brigade—shot my great-great-great grandfather Winslow Walker in the back of the head in cold blood. It's only recently that the truth of this sordid event came to my attention. Apparently, there was a feud of some kind. I'm afraid I have become consumed by revenge. I know it's not becoming of a gentleman to seek petty reprisals, but this is a matter of family honor. I'm sure if you were in my position, you'd do the same, Mr. Ford.'

'You're crazy, you can't do this.'

'Men like me can do what we wish, Mr. Ford,' said Walker, laughing above the wind which was beginning to rise again.

'I thought you knew that.'

I took a couple of deep breaths and recalled times I'd escaped from tight spots. Admittedly, none were this precarious, but I had to do something. I decided to run, preferring to be shot trying to escape than resigning myself to certain death. It was in then I was struck by the horrific thought perhaps Walker intended to bury me alive. Maybe he would shoot me but not kill me and leave me in the box to linger in agony. My mind filled with the unimaginable terror of being trapped and slowly suffocating. Over the years of working for men like Walker, I had learned another truth about them. I learned how for many of them, cruelty was part of their nature and in matters of revenge, no matter how convoluted, the cruelty was the point. I determined if I were to die, it would be quick. I leaned forward and put my hands on the ground.

'That's right, you stay there like a dog,' said Walker.

I readied my weight for forward movement. I had no idea how easy it would be for Walker to shoot, the only thing I knew was he did not expect me to run. Walker had lived his whole life in control of every situation he'd found himself in, and there was no reason for him to think this was any different. I slid my right leg along the dirt and lifted my ankle, so the ball of my foot was bearing my weight.

When Walker didn't react, I knew he hadn't noticed, and without hesitation I pushed off and sped into the pitch black as fast as my muscles would let me. A gunshot rang out, and a bullet whistled by my ear, followed by another shot which didn't seem as close. I surged forward with my legs already burning from the

Robert McDermott

effort, and within a matter of seconds I was in the labyrinth of boulders. I ran into a wall of solid stone and fell.

I jumped up to find myself surrounded by wisps of light and shadow. Shapes began to form in the air, and from them faces pushed at me as if emerging from underwater. I saw men with thick whiskers and cold eyes. They were everywhere. The dead's guttural screams bounced off the rocks and echoed into the starless sky.

I ran, tumbling into nothingness; I had no idea where I was going. I had no idea where Walker was. I didn't care. Pursued by the shapes and sounds of the past, I ran through one turn after another, maybe making headway, maybe not. Maybe I ran in circles.

But I kept running. South-west, south, south-east, east…

# MOSSY BRENNAN'S ROAD TO DAMASCUS

In the months leading up to the destruction of Flaherty's pub, Mossy Brennan spent his nights in fitful pockets of sleep. It was unseasonably warm. Mossy would toss and turn before unpeeling his dry tongue from the roof of his mouth and swearing. Then Herself in the bed beside him would wake and hit him a slap. She'd tell him to go off into the spare room, and then he'd suggest they engage in marital relations. Mostly she'd hit him another slap, and he'd trudge off to the spare room, but on the odd occasion when she agreed, Mossy, delighted with himself, would need no second invitation, and afterward, he'd sleep as soundly as he ever did, even when the humidity was as thick as the skin of an old pig.

Then one night, much to his consternation and embarrassment, he found himself wanting.

'You're tired,' said Herself, 'go back to sleep.'

'I'm not tired,' said Mossy.

'Then it's the drink.'

'I only had a few.'

'Doesn't matter the reason, you can get something for it down at Hickey's.'

'What do you mean?'

'You know, pills, the little blue ones.'

'Arra, go away with that,' he said, dismissing the idea.

When it happened a second time and then a third, she took the matter out of his hands, as it were, and stormed off to Hickey's to explain the situation. She was hoping to speak to Rosemary, but Old Man Hickey was on duty and when he asked Herself what she wanted, she panicked. Then, in that odd way panic works, instead of running from the shop like a scalded cat, she stood there listening to the words coming from her mouth in unfathomable astonishment.

'Mossy can't do his duty as a husband,' she said, trying to hold back the tears.

While it was no secret Herself and Mossy had no children, Old Man Hickey had to mull over her words for a moment before he understood what she meant. He pushed his glasses up his nose, for they had slid down when his mouth had fallen open. He had no idea what to say. In all his years dispensing remedies, he'd never had a woman utter those words to him. Eventually, he told her they didn't stock what she wanted and suggested she get what she needed off the computer and then take confession from Fr. Lacey.

'Why would I need confession?'

'The Lord sees all your sins,' said Old Man Hickey, staring her down.

'What sins are you talking about?' she said, hands on hips and defiant.

Old Man Hickey shuffled off into the dispensary at the back and closed the door.

She didn't confess, but she did go online to order a box of little blue lozenges. These promptly arrived in a discrete package. O'Dowd the postman must have known what was in the package because he gave her the filthies when she opened the door to him. She got similar looks down at the local shop and at the hairdressers, but it was nothing compared to what Mossy experienced at Flaherty's the night it burned to the ground.

Since Herself had gone to Hickey's he'd not been to Flaherty's pub. For three evenings in a row, he drove the five miles to Riordan's over the hill. When Herself saw the state of his parking the next morning, she hid the keys and told him if he wanted a jar, he'd have to go to Flaherty's.

'I can't, you've ruined me. Old Man Hickey will be there and Fr. Lacey and sure, how would I look Fionnula in the eye and ask her for a pint?'

'You're being dramatic.'

'Fr. Lacey will say it's a judgment from God. I'll be a pariah.'

'Enough with that nonsense, Mossy, now get yourself down there this evening, or do I have to drag you by the ear?'

She'd started a new box set on Netflix and was really getting into it. She planned to watch it all evening and didn't want him moping around.

He approached Flaherty's like a reluctant dog called to heel. The evening was drawing a redness in the west, and the sun shimmered on the hilltops. It had taken him almost two hours to get to the pub, and he couldn't properly recollect his journey. He'd left home just after dinner. Herself was on the couch with a big box of Celebrations and a glass of Malbec the size of a fishbowl.

'And don't mind any of them,' she said as he put on his cap and snuck out the door like a thief.

Her voice was ringing in his head as he nipped in the door of the snug. There was a good crowd and while this gave him decent odds of going unnoticed for a few minutes, it also meant once he was noticed he'd be like a badger surrounded by hounds.

Old Man Hickey and Fr. Lacey were there. As soon as Mossy entered the twilight world, he locked eyes with the pair of them and froze. There was a silence like the beginning of time, and Mossy turned to beat a hasty retreat when Tom Hanlon came in through the door behind him, blocking his exit. Tom, a genial man and not at all given to hearsay, smiled broadly at Mossy and clapped his hands on Mossy's shoulders.

'Are you well, Mossy?' he said loudly.

Mossy was sure as birds laid eggs, Tom had shouted the greeting and that all in sundry had heard and were whispering about him.

'Not bad, Tom.'

'Are you staying or going?'

Before Mossy could answer, Tom had pulled him towards the bar and had roared Fionnula's name. About a minute later, she appeared, looking busy but unflustered. A checked towel was draped over her arm. She began to wipe down the bar before addressing Tom.

'Two pints,' said Tom.

Fionnula nodded and gave Mossy a friendly smile. Mossy tried to reciprocate, but his heart was pounding.

'I heard you were in Riordan's the past few nights,' said Fionnula.

She put the pints on the drainer to settle.

'I was trying to sell the bull,' said Mossy, looking down at his hands.

Fionnula gave him a quizzical look. He was trying to hold it together by not breathing through his mouth. Fionnula placed the pints before them and returned to the main bar without another word.

Tom lifted his pint, appreciating its uniform aesthetic, and then took a drink. Mossy barely managed a sip.

'How long have you got that bull?'

'A year,' said Mossy.

'He's a shorthorn, if I'm not mistaken?'

'Charolais.'

'I was sure he was a shorthorn.'

Mossy looked around the snug involuntarily. Old Man Hickey sat there, as quiet and unmoving as a gravestone. Fr. Lacey was nowhere to be seen. Mossy's mind was racing with questions. He was sure Tom knew the breed of his bull, and yet, he had given the wrong answer. Was he mocking me? Mossy wondered. He was, but that wasn't Tom's way. He shook his head and took a drink.

'What's the matter?' said Tom.

'What do you mean?' said Mossy.

'With the bull. You'd be hoping to get more than a year, didn't you pay a good price for him?'

'I did, but he's a bit wild.'

'Sure they're all wild, did the vet take a look at him?'

'He did.'

'And?'

Tom leaned in close. His big red face loomed over Mossy like a desert sun.

'Tell me this, Mossy,' said Tom, whispering, 'is he still up to the job, you know up to the job?'

Mossy almost spilled his pint.

'I'd not be selling him if he wasn't,' said Mossy belligerently.

Tom laughed and clapped Mossy hard on the back.

'No better man, Mossy.'

Mossy reeled from the force of Tom's slap and took a deep breath. He coughed and then brought his pint to his mouth and drank about half of it in one gulp.

'You'll have another, won't you?' said Tom.

Fionnula, having heard Tom's bellow, appeared once again into the snug and poured two more pints. With the finishing of the first pint and the head taken off the second, Mossy felt the stiff edge of anxiety leave him like a cool breeze rising from a lake. He was immeasurably grateful Tom had fallen for his lies about the bull, and was now engaging Fionnula in a bit of non-sense about something or other. He reckoned he'd have this pint and then perhaps another and that'd be it. He knew Herself had the pills at the ready in the bedside locker, and he knew he'd be taking one whether he liked it or not. She always got amorous after she'd watched a romantic boxset. Normally, it was awful stuff about serial killers or lawyers, but this one had a strapping young lad in it which was sure to get things going. Thoughts about the bull, amongst other things, were tumbling through his mind when a firm prod on the point of his elbow shook him from his cogitations.

'I hear you went to Riordan's over the hill.'

It was Fr. Lacey. His tinted glasses, dark garb, and shiny shoes gave him the look of the Gestapo. Mossy became flustered again, it was one thing telling Tom a fib about why he sought the embrace of Riordan's, but he couldn't lie to a man of the cloth, especially not one as intimidating as Fr. Lacey.

'Yes, Father,' was all Mossy could bumble. He felt like a schoolboy being admonished by the headmaster.

'Do you know the story of St. Paul's conversion?'

Fr. Lacey's glasses had become even darker. Mossy couldn't look at him. He pulled his pint to his mouth, trying to keep his hand steady.

'Saul of Tarsus,' said Fr. Lacey, 'was on the road to Damascus when suddenly a light from heaven flashed around him, and he heard a voice asking Saul, why do you persecute me?'

Mossy kept his eyes on the little bubbles on the top of his pint. He thought they looked like little craters on the moon.

'Look at me, Mossy,' said Fr. Lacey loudly.

Mossy, shaken to his foundations, turned slowly to face the clergyman.

'He was struck blind, Mossy, for three days the Lord scourged him. He burned the sin from his eyes. Do you understand me, Mossy?'

Mossy hadn't a notion about what this fearful man was trying to impart to him, but he nodded nevertheless. Fr. Lacey prodded him heavily on the shoulder, and Mossy felt the electric flex in the nerve of his arm, which made his hand twitch. He jerked spasmodically and spilled the rest of his pint. Fionnula took the towel from her arm and wiped up the mess.

'Stay with your own flock, Mossy. The sheep who strays becomes lost and ends up eaten by the wolf.'

'I'm sorry, Father, it won't happen again.'

Fr. Lacey uttered something in Latin and blessed Mossy, and sat back down beside Old Hickey.

Fionnula put a fresh pint in front of Mossy, but he didn't notice. He was having a flashback of some kind. Fr. Lacey's words about the light from heaven had rung a bell in his memory. There was a long white light with purple at the edges. He was about two miles from home on the descending side of the hills when he saw it out his lefthand side. It was disc-shaped and made a weird humming noise like the fridge did from time to time. It was going wild fast, and he put the foot down. After that, he didn't remember anything except he'd got home, and the car was parked arseways.

'You're miles away, Mossy. Is it a nice daydream you're having?'

Her voice was friendly and suggested understanding. Mossy took a satisfying gulp from his pint and as soon as the bitter taste tingled the back of his tongue, he remembered the rest of it. It wasn't Riordan's he was leaving from. It was Flaherty's. It was the night he'd had his performance-related issue. A vivid timeline of events materialised in his thoughts as clear as June morning. He'd had a few pints, certainly no more. He was fixing the roof on the bull's shed the next day and certainly couldn't do work like with a head on him. He got in the car and began the short drive home. He remembered that the eejit was on the radio again and fiddling with the dial to get rid of his stupid voice. It was while he was doing this that the light appeared at the car's side. Next thing he knew, he was home. He was demented by the heat and the strangeness of everything, not to mention Herself going on about the pills.

Mossy drank his pint in one mouthful, like a gull swallowing a swag-bellied rat. He slammed the empty glass on the counter and stood up with the emphatic rigidity of a statesman.

'Bastards,' he said furiously.

'What is it, Mossy?' said Tom.

'They stole my dignity, the bastards.'

'Mind your language, Mossy,' said Fr. Lacey.

Mossy's face illuminated in a raging crimson. He stared at Fr. Lacey with a demented intensity. Fr. Lacey frowned in quizzical bemusement.

'Fuck off you, ya bockety poxbottle,' said Mossy realising all his fury in a single uninhibited growl like a caged tiger, 'this is your fault, you and your St. Paul and the three days of blindness. Instead of going blind, I've had my manhood struck down.'

The stunned silence in the snug was the kind you'd hear even the thought of a pin dropping. Fr. Lacey peered over his glasses and then like a hungry greyhound he barrelled out of his seat and went for Mossy with savage ferocity. Mossy barely made it out the door. As he ran into the dark, he could hear the flaring of Fr. Lacey's nostrils as he tore up the ground between them. The next he knew he'd been caught, and Fr. Lacey was on him.

'What did you call me, you little bollix?' he roared in a chaotic fury of slaps and kicks.

Mossy tried his best to fend them off. Luckily for him, the priest was about as coordinated as a drunk giraffe.

'I'll have you excommunicated, you filthy delinquent, I'll write to the bishop, you'll be cast into the wilderness like a pagan.'

By now, a decent crowd had gathered. Mossy and Fr. Lacey's confrontation was illuminated by the big moon, and the limbs of ancient hazels and birches and hawthorns formed a wonderfully dramatic backdrop to the most entertaining thing the patrons of Flaherty's had seen since Ray Houghton's goal against England in the '88 Euros.

'I'll have a tenner on Fr. Lacey,' said a voice from the back.

'I'll take that bet,' said another.

Before long, a book was open, and money began to exchange hands.

Mossy had grabbed a stray branch as a weapon and Fr. Lacey was giving it a whole Bruce Lee routine. He let out a loud shriek and launched himself at Mossy, leading with his leg. Fr. Lacey was mid-flight like a ninja when Mossy caught him squarely in the groin with the pointy end of the branch. The priest collapsed in a crumpled heap like an old tent. There was an audible gasp from the assembled crowd, followed by a few sympathetic groans from the men.

'Right in the clackers.'

'Just as well he's a priest.'

While Fr. Lacey lay on the ground stunned, the breath sheared from him, the pain yet to fully register, an intense light cut through the darkness.

Mossy pointed the branch at the light.

'What in the name of Jaysus is that?' said Tom.

Old Man Hickey had shuffled off down the road. All this commotion was too much for him, and besides, he reckoned he'd get no more conversation from Fr. Lacey. He was mulling over whether to tell the priest about Herself and the fornication pills, but now that Mossy had opened the holy man with the end of a pointy branch, Old Man Hickey reasoned the assault on Fr. Lacey had put Mossy's soul in greater peril than any amount of carnal desire could.

The light which was moving slowly towards them. It was a wide oblong shape, and it made a low humming noise like a fridge. A violet hue rippled along its edges, making it resemble a jellyfish. By now, Mossy's nerves were so frayed, he decided to go all Basil Fawlty and charged at the light, waving the branch above his head and screaming like a berserker.

'What's Mossy doing?'

The question remained unanswered. All at once, there was a rumbling noise followed by a loud pop. A line of intense purple light shot from the object, taking the top off Mossy's branch and blowing a six-foot hole in the pub's upper floor. Mossy hit the ground, and everyone scattered into the night like mice at the hoot of an owl. Thankfully, everyone was outside when the pub caught fire.

The light hovered over Mossy for a moment and though he was terrified beyond the rational, he felt a warming glow flood through his body. It then moved over to Fr. Lacey stopped a moment, and then it was gone high over the trees and the hills like a comet. The patrons of Riordan's saw a light shoot into the night sky and marvelled for a time.

Mossy stood up; he looked around him in bewilderment. To his right, Fr. Lacey got slowly to his feet. He was a little unsteady at first, but soon enough had the steady surefootedness of a goat. Mossy regarded the priest from a safe distance.

'Are you injured, Father?'

The priest patted himself down and made a discreet gentleman's adjustment.

'It would appear not.'

'It's a miracle,' quipped Mossy.

The priest shot him a frown which seared his eyes.

'I'm not in the humour for such nonsense, Mossy.'

'No hard feelings, Father,' said Mossy in a meek and contrite voice.

Fr. Lacey turned to him and moved a few steps closer. The frame of Flaherty's was beginning to collapse, and the flames rose into the dark like rose petals.

'You'll be taking confession one of these days, I trust?'

'Indeed, I will, Father, most definitely.'

'You'll bring Herself with you?'

'I will.'

'Goodnight, Mossy.'

'Goodnight, Father.'

The priest took heavy steps on the soft ground. His shoes were filthy. He'd need a lot of polish to get them spick and span. In addition, it looked like he'd need to visit the Specsavers on Main Street. Mossy wondered if he'd be sent a bill along with the monthly contribution envelope. It didn't matter just then. Mossy headed home. Somewhere in the dark, sheep bleated, and a pheasant shrieked.

As he approached his house, Mossy caught a scent on the air. He knew it intimately, but it had never been this strong before. He noticed the light was on in the front room. Herself would be up and watching her box set. A renewed sense of vigour surged through him, and he strode purposefully to the front door. Before going in, he slapped his hands together as if he were about to tuck into a good meal.

'Grand job', he said to himself as he turned the handle.

# BOATS AGAINST THE CURRENT

It was the trail of her scarf, like the rhythmic movement of a sea-anemone, which caught my eye. Trinity College mid-October with me only passing through on my way somewhere else. Long odds, or fate, though that was itself a longer shot. Either way, it happened, and I didn't want to miss the opportunity. I glimpsed her face in the crowd and lost every other detail except the wheat-yellow scarf signalling to me. It was both seductive and ambiguous, like a word within a whispered sentence. Could it be the same scarf, I wondered. I followed, or at least tried to. Moving among the threshing throng and keeping eyes on her was difficult. I narrowly avoided bumping into people and the whole time C3PO's voice rattled in my head telling me the possibility of successfully navigating an asteroid field is approximately 3,720-1. Stupid nerd stuff always came to mind, to *my* mind anyway. It was one of the many reasons I had a hard time in school. I pushed my way through the thick wall of bodies and snatched conversation and would have lost her but for her stopping just before leaving the Arts Building. She was looking at her phone. She put it away quickly, but it was enough for me to refocus.

In that moment, when I could see her the most clearly, I hesitated. Was it her, could I have mistaken her for someone else, was I following her more in hope than expectation? It had been eight years and an entire adolescence since we'd last spoken. There was a lot of room for error, as my father would say. I opened my mouth to call her name, but all that came out was a click of strangled words. A heavy-set guy with a strong Limerick accent asked what my problem was and that I was a right dope. There were giggles from his company, and I felt a familiar heat rising in my face. I moved away and rushed from the Arts Building and towards The Quad. She was heading towards Regent House, and I knew if she got out onto College Green before I could catch up, I was sure I'd lose her in the city's bustle.

'Now everybody, this is Kate Molloy,' said Mrs. Bradshaw, our form teacher. I was thirteen, and my eyes lifting and landing on the new girl was like water rinsing away the final dust of my childhood. I felt a sudden pleasing lightness and readjusted my legs under the desk and sat with the quiet amazement you some-times see on the faces of people at the theatre or galleries. *Kate Molloy*, the sound of her name found a place in my mind like a bird flying into the upper reaches of a belltower. 'Kate has moved here from Newbridge in County Kildare,' said Mrs. Brad-shaw, 'tell them about yourself Kate. Go on, girl, don't be so meek.'

It was then, that exact moment where every star in the galaxy conspired, and Kate Molloy looked directly at me, making me feel as if I were the only person in the world. 'I like horses,' she said, 'and I like hockey and I like Madonna.' Her voice was high and a little nasal, as if she were pinching it slightly. Three girls down the back of the class giggled in unison. One of them said something derogatory about hockey, but Kate Molloy, despite her nervousness, carried on undeterred. She told us how her fa-ther had been offered a job in Dublin. I could have listened to her all day. To me, her voice sounded like it had come from the top of a mountain, bringing with it sheer air to pierce my soul. 'Has anyone got a question for Kate?' asked Mrs. Bradshaw. There was total quiet. I wondered why everyone was looking at me. 'Are you going to ask your question Mr. Kelly or is your hand being moved by some unseen forces of which we are not aware?'

Mrs. Bradshaw's voice had the echoey reverberation of sound in a dream. Kate Molloy's eyes fixed on me. I thought I saw the flicker of a smile. 'What colour is your horse?' I asked. 'Grey,' she said, 'he's a grey named Gandalf.'

For three months, Kate Molloy and I shared no other words. The girls who giggled at her interest in horses and hockey welcomed her into their clique within a week and soon afterward, the boys in second and third year began to take note of her, revelling in her shiny hair, gregarious nature and willingness to laugh at their stupid jokes.

Just before the Christmas holidays, she passed me a note in English telling me she had liked my poem. I had written something I thought was deep and meaningful for an assignment and when Mr. Merrill coerced me into reading it aloud to the class I barely managed to get it out. The effect of my hesitancy and the poem's title What's it all about? Combined to produce a cacophony of heckling laughter culminating in Sean Morrisey saying 'What's it all about? It's about time Kelly shut up.' I saw Mr. Merrill chuckle to himself before turning on his teacher's face and reprimanding Morrissey. It was too late; the damage had been done. I was marked as an outcast and would never return to the unobtrusive shadows from where I'd come.

The next day, Kate Molloy's note heaped more misery on my already fragile state. It read *your poem was really good, I hope you write more* and while I was over the moon she had taken the time to tell me that, it came with the realisation, the powerful and immediate realisation that I couldn't share it with anyone, that it had to remain secret and therefore deepen my isolation.

There were no more poems or notes after that, and every time I looked at Kate Molloy, she was unaware of it or ignored me. At least once or twice a day, I'd pass by her and her friends. Sometimes there'd be a teasing comment about my poem and sometimes there'd be giggling, but every time I walked by, Kate Molloy's face was turned or obscured in some way. Once I had passed them, I never dared to look back. Several times I thought to shove her note into the giggling mob's faces, but I knew it was a last resort and would have the same effect as smashing a glass ornament with a hammer. And so, the distant, one-sided affection continued until just before the end of the school year.

I heard through a fellow outcast, Kate Molloy was moving back to Kildare. I decided I had to act, but had no idea how. If I was bold, it could backfire and make things worse and if I were timid, I would be eaten alive. As it turned out, an opportunity came my way. We were in science class about two weeks before the summer break and I found myself at a sink cleaning a conical flask when she moved in beside me. She smiled and said 'move over' in a playful way before indicating she wanted to clean her flask. The sun reflected in her eyes, and I almost dropped my flask. It slipped like it was covered in oil, but I managed to grab it before it hit the sink's cold surface. 'I'm going to miss this place,' she said before delivering a bombshell which scrambled my mind. 'I'm having a party next weekend to say goodbye to everyone, and I'd like you to come,' she said in a perfectly sincere tone. My instincts were to consider her invitation a cruel prank engineered by one or all the giggling mob. Her eyes widened as I stared at her. 'Don't think too hard about it,' she said with a hint of incredulity. 'Sorry,' I said, and then added a hasty, 'I'll be there.' 'Good,' she said, 'I'm looking forward to it.' She moved closer, nudging me aside with her hips. I dropped my flask. Luckily, it didn't crack, but the noise and subsequent wobbling rattle brought Mr. Byrne over to the sink to lecture me about being careful with laboratory equipment. By the time he was through with me, Kate Molloy had returned to her seat.

The party was awful. There were too many people and I only got to speak to Kate once when I gave her a wheat-yellow scarf as a gift. She was flanked by the giggling girls and as she opened the box one of them said 'who gives someone a scarf in the summer?' Kate gave me a half smile and said thanks. They were the last words I heard from her. I moved around the house for a short time, but there was no-one I knew, and after trying and failing to catch Kate alone, I gave up and called my dad to bring me home. Just before he arrived, I was sure I saw Kate go down to the back of the darkening garden with a boy from the Junior Cup team. On my way out of the house, I saw the scarf lying on the floor in the hallway, exactly where Kate Molloy and her friends had been standing when I had presented it to her. I felt an impulse to pick it up, but Kate's mother called me and the chance was gone. My dad was full of chat, and he and Kate's mother yapped for a few minutes about whatever nonsense adults felt necessary to say to one another in social situations. I stood there dutifully waiting for them to finish. All the time my eyes were on the scarf. On the way home, dad continued to blab on, but I barely spoke, preferring to look out the window at the last light being sucked from the evening.

I upped my pace as I got to Regent House and almost ran into a tourist who said, 'goddamn, watch it, son.' I apologised to him, but he had already moved along. The doorway to College Green was busy with other tourists, and I had to be polite but firm as I made my way through. I saw the scarf flickering in the fading October light. She was heading towards Grafton Street. I was beginning to formulate questions and a conversation in my head *… are you studying in Trinity? No, I'm out in DCU … where are you based in the city? Wow, I'm not too far from there … have you plans for later? Are you free now?*

It was within the pleasurable mix of nostalgia and anticipation, a claw of doubt grabbed my gut and wrenched me from my daydream. Suppose it was her, would she recognise me and if she did, would she want to talk? After all, we had barely shared a hundred words during the year we were classmates. Was that all it would come to, a hesitant hi and a vacant look or sorry, I thought you were someone else? I pushed the rising fear into the deeper reaches of my being and followed the scarf, which was now a faint Willo-the-Wisp in the tumult of autumnal colour surrounding it.

'Did you enjoy the party?' asked my dad. I shrugged and continued looking into the thickening dusk. 'Her mother said they're moving back because they couldn't really settle in Dublin.

Sometimes it happens to people who aren't used to cities, they find it hard to get used to the noise and the pace.'

I said nothing.

'Sure,' said my dad after we passed through the disco glow of another set of traffic lights, 'why don't you ask her for her address or phone number when you see her in school next week, maybe you could keep in touch?'

I looked at him with the sort of disdain only a teenager can muster.

'It's just a thought,' he added.

The rest of the journey was conducted in near silence but for my dad reaching across and tousling my hair.

'Don't feel too bad,' he said, 'you'll have many nights like this.'

I was less than ten feet away from her. I had dispelled almost all doubt. There was a stillness in the air, as if before rain. She was matching my pace, but I pushed forward now, sensing how timing would be key.

I turned to face my dad. 'How many?' I asked.

He chuckled.

'God knows.'

His chuckle made me feel worse.

I don't know what compelled me to grab the scarf. Maybe because I was so close, maybe because my mind was preoccupied with a muddle of excitement and my heart felt like it was trying to make its way into my mouth. My fingers inched ahead of my moving body and in my imagination mirrored the scarf's fluttering tassels. Two hands about to touch. I reached and felt its smooth softness on my fingertips, and then as soon as I held it, it was gone.

*Who gives someone a scarf in the summer?* The comment's tone is reproachful and sardonic. *Maybe you'd like to read your poem, Mr. Kelly? Get up there and share your wisdom with us, I don't care if you don't want to.*

I'm sure Mr. Merrill was in on it.

*Yeah, that's a stupid gift,* someone says as I retreat into a shell of embarrassment. I turn and move away and despite telling myself not to, I look back and see the scarf fall to the floor, folding on top of itself like a gymnast's ribbon. I get a glimpse of Kate's face, but it is obscured by the baying pack. I turn away once more and as I do her head moves in my direction. Our opposite movements are so precisely in tune, like gears moving in a machine or stars rotating around the centre of a galaxy, which I never see the look in her eyes telling me how she wished things could be different.

# 6EQUJ5, THANK YOU VERY MUCH!

My father worked on the bomb at Los Alamos in the 1940s. He was an assistant to the boss man, Oppenheimer, and would sometimes sit in meetings with Manley and Fermi and Feynman and all the other physicists determined to open the atom and see what was inside. Their research was under military brass's close eye. There was a lot of pressure to stop the Nazis before they engulfed the world with their twisted vision. The grapevine at the time suggested the Germans were ahead of the game, so you'll appreciate the sense of urgency was pretty high.

In the wake of Pearl Harbor, Roosevelt sanctioned the bomb's development, and my father found himself involved in the war effort despite failing the draft on account of his eyes. If you want to imagine what my father looked like, think skinny button-down plaid shirt nerd with glasses thick as milk bottles.

So, they began work on the bomb, which would eventually lead to their kind of world peace. Funny how making a bomb with the potential to destroy the world could lead to peace. The history books may tell a story about heroism and how the world was purged of evil and all that noble stuff, but that's not the entire truth, is it? History is full of weird shit and unintended consequences.

This story isn't one you've heard before. It concerns the weird shit and unintended consequences which arose from tinkering about in the cosmic toolbox. In some ways, this might be the most important story in human history, but you can decide for yourself.

The Manhattan Project was beyond top secret, and no one knew the whole picture. My father knew about as much as a one-eyed man looking at the night sky through broken binoculars. He helped Oppenheimer with fast neutron calculations, but don't ask me what they are. Strangely enough, considering how smart my father was, I just about got through remedial math, but then again, I was good at sports and my father couldn't throw a baseball further than his nose.

During our childhood, my sister and I would hear stories about Pop's time in the desert working on the bomb. I didn't care much for all the science stuff. It was boring, and I never fully shook the idea my father was a nerd. He would sometimes tell us about the other scientists. I liked the fact Richard Feynman would go into the wilderness and play bongos for days on end. Can you imagine a Nobel Laureate, possibly one of the greatest scientific minds ever, going into the New Mexico desert to play bongos in his downtime? They called him *Injun Joe*. Pop said Feynman was the funniest guy he'd ever met. I found it difficult to put funny and science together, but I took him at his word. I saw a recording of Feynman a while back. He was lecturing on the scientific method and people were laughing, so maybe he was funny, or maybe it was easier to make people laugh back then. Mom corroborated Pop's opinion, but instead of saying Feynman was funny, she said he was charming.

My parents didn't meet until after Pop left Los Alamos. Feynman was at their wedding, so was Oppenheimer. Apparently, a few of Hoover's goons turned up too. Joe McCarthy had people seeing commies everywhere, and Oppenheimer was under suspicion for some opinions he'd expressed years before. Regardless of this, it was a great day by all accounts. It was probably the night my sister was conceived. I arrived a year later. I reckon my folks had us quickly since my father was exposed to all that radiation in the desert and who knew what it had done to his junk.

Ultimately, it was radiation which did for him. He spent all of his working life in and around science labs and died of cancer aged fifty-eight in late spring of 1978.

We didn't speak much until the last year of his life.

We shared a certain taciturn quality, and our idea of spending time with one another was going to the movies. We'd sit quietly and afterward, he'd say 'good movie' or 'I didn't care for it so much' and I'd drive him home, and he'd say goodnight and I'd say goodnight and that was about it. There were lots of great movies at the time, but none greater than *Star Wars,* which came out in late May 1977. I loved all those B-Movies from the 50s and 60s, and *Star Wars* promised to take things to the next level. From the moment the iconic music blared through the auditorium and the crawler began unfurling on the screen, I was hooked. Pop, on the other hand, hated it. He sat in the theatre shaking his head and cribbing about things and generally being a nuisance. Later, in the car, he kept calling it unrealistic garbage and muttered 'it's not like that, it's not like that at all.' I didn't pay much attention to him. He was on medication for his cancer, and frankly I was annoyed at him. The following week, we saw *Smokey and the Bandit.*

Anyway, in November he called me up and told me he wanted to see *Close Encounters of the Third Kind*, and he'd something to tell me. I was reluctant at first but also surprised. 'You hate those movies, remember *Star Wars*?' I said to him on the phone. 'So?' he said before adding, 'you can pick me up at seven.' As I hung up, my wife reminded me, there wasn't much time and I should try to enjoy what was left.

The movie was good, but it didn't have the laser blaster coolness of Han Solo or the sinister dread of Darth Vader. It was a much more intellectual movie, and Pop sat through the whole thing without so much as a peep out of him. He was quiet on the way home too, and when we got to his house, he told me to come in. It wasn't an invitation. Pop may have been a nerd, but he'd spent his life around military men and knew how to talk like them. I followed him sheepishly. It was already a little late, and I had to work the next day, but I couldn't refuse.

Entering my childhood home, the passage of time became acute. There were pictures of me and my sister and the various dogs and cats which shared our childhood. Mom was asleep, and Pop told me to grab a beer from the fridge and follow him into the study.

The study was an oak-panelled room with a couple of leather armchairs and a big Maplewood desk which I would eventually inherit and put my back out trying to carry into the study where I'm typing these words. Pop didn't drink much as it messed with his medication, but on this occasion, he poured himself a whisky from a bottle he kept in the desk.

'That was a good movie,' he said, taking a sip.

I nodded. I knew if I spoke, he'd rattle on, either agreeing with or challenging me.

'Much better than that space western crap we saw in May.'

He was trying to push my buttons. I held firm. After about thirty seconds of icy silence, he gave up.

'Well, I suppose I'd better get to the reason I invited you in,' he said.

He spoke for about twenty minutes straight about splitting the atom and how it was, at the time, mankind's greatest scientific achievement. I was bored stiff. Only after his lecture did he get to something interesting.

'Setting off the bomb was what got their attention,' he said.

'The Japanese?' I said flatly.

'No you dumb cracker,' he said, 'the space aliens, like the ones in the movie we saw tonight.'

I wanted to say to him how medication and the booze were not a good mix, but he was so earnest. I sat back and listened as he continued.

He said the 'space aliens' had been in the neighbourhood for a while, monitoring the growth of our civilisation. He referenced stuff like the Nazca Lines and things from the ancient world, which implied alien technology. I was expecting George Lucas to come in through the door and say it was all a joke, but Pop's words had a compelling authority to them. He said our relationship with the aliens was kinda like the relationship of a kid with an ant farm. We were a curiosity to them and not much else.

'Then, at 5:29 a.m. on July 16th, 1945, when they exploded the Trinity bomb,' he said, 'it all changed.'

'How?'

He rubbed his grizzled chin and took another sip of his second whisky, and in a peculiarly remote voice he said, 'it was as if ants in the ant farm had suddenly learned to speak and their message was loud and clear.'

'What was the message?'

'Don't screw with us,' said Pop.

He didn't say anything else that night, but every week after our movie he'd tell me a little more about the story, leading with the bomb or something from Los Alamos before going all Carl Sagan mystic on me.

He told me how the morning they tested the bomb at Trinity, the New Mexico desert shone with a light as bright as a million suns, and how a huge mushroom cloud loomed over them like a primordial beast. He said it was like nothing he could put into words, except it was as close as he got to a religious experience which didn't involve personal things with Mom. He said there was a tremendous sense of triumph immediately after the test, but the biggest emotion was relief. The mood in private was different. Oppenheimer kept shuffling around the lab saying we had become the destroyer of worlds and how it was all very bad indeed.

Three weeks later, on August 6th, they dropped Little Boy on Hiroshima, and three days after, Fat Man took out Nagasaki. The military boys were smoking cigars and drinking expensive booze and giving one another slaps on the back. They had won. The scientists understood that for the conqueror the end justified the means, but for many of them, it left a bad taste. The war wrapped up pretty quick afterward. Truman gave Oppenheimer the Medal of Merit in 1946. The nuclear age had begun. Optimism abounded. Certainly, there was no talk of aliens. Until the real close encounter of the third kind at Roswell in 1947.

'It's all about the number seven,' said Pop the following week. We'd been to see *Semi-tough*. Pop liked Burt Reynolds, describing him as a 'cool dude'. Even in my late twenties, I cringed when my father used the parlance of the times. The worst was after he'd seen Shaft. I was still living at home at the time and recalled the acute embarrassment Pop's behaviour caused. He'd be shaving and singing *who's the black private dick that's a sex machine to all the chicks*, expecting me to join in with the refrain. It was so out of character for him, but then again, as he got older, he got odder and odder.

'All the big events happened in a year ending in seven.'

'What about the moon landing?

He waved his hand at my comment, dismissing it with disdain.

'In 47' a UFO came down in the desert outside Roswell, New Mexico', he said.

'In 57' the Russians put Sputnik in orbit.'

Pop paused and a flicker of something I'd not seen in a while flashed across his face.

'After Sputnik, they put a dog in space. The first sentient creature to be put in orbit. Her name was Laika. She was a sweet pooch.'

'Okay,' I said slowly, wondering what he was leading up to.

'67' was the year it all went south.'

'What do you mean?'

'So many accidents,' he said, after a moment.

He scratched the side of his face. In the light, his gaunt features were exacerbated. His clothes hung loosely on his thin frame, and his eyes were sunken. His voice, however, remained resonant and deep. Had you only heard Pop's voice, you'd have pictured someone entirely different.

'First, there was the Apollo 11 fire in January, then there was the Soyuz crash in April, and later in the year, there were four or five accidents involving test planes. It was a mess. They were going to shut it all down.'

'Why didn't they?' I asked.

'As far as the public were concerned, it was all about national pride,' he began, 'it was a race to beat the Russians and a debt to Jack Kennedy who'd promised to put a man on the moon. Which was a big waste of money if you ask me.'

He paused from his story and pointed his finger at me in a playful way. A smile spread across his thin lips.

'The truth about the Space Race wasn't about national pride or any other hogwash. It was about preparedness. We were expecting the little green men who'd announced themselves to us in '47' to come back.'

'The Roswell crash.'

'Yep.'

'Did they find anything?'

'Not exactly.'

'Ok, this year is almost over,' I said, feeling clever, 'what's the big event of 1977?'

He got out of his chair and shuffled over to the record player. His movements were stiff. It looked like he was taking a great effort to sift through the stack of vinyl beside the player.

'I always liked Hank Williams; you know that, don't you?'

I didn't need to answer, it wasn't a question. The warble of Williams' voice formed aspects of my childhood's soundtrack. Bars of *I'm so Lonesome I could Die* and *Cold Cold Heart* ripped through me like electricity. I was hoping he wasn't going to play Hank Williams.

'I didn't care too much for rock n' roll, always preferred Hank and Johnny and Merle and those boys.'

The melancholic tones of *Are you Lonesome Tonight* crackled from the speakers.

'I thought Mom was the Elvis fan,' I said.

Pop shuffled away from the record player and sank back into his seat. I expected him to break into pieces. The music was soft and low enough to speak over.

'There's a guy I know over at OSU, he runs the Big Ear telescope for SETI.'

I'd no idea what he was talking about. For a moment, I thought he was having a stroke. He gave me the coldest deadeye stare and then shook his head.

'Have you ever read a newspaper?' he said, and before I could object, he carried on.

'The Big Ear is a radio telescope at Ohio State. It's scanning the sky for signals from outer space.'

He spoke to me like I was an imbecile.

'After Roswell, there were side projects around the new-found knowledge of how we were not alone. The first thing they did was suppress all leaks. Nothing could get out. Then they created a screen of disinformation, allowing for plausible deniability. Truman didn't even know about it.'

'So, how did it get out?'

He squeezed his eyes together and blinked as if to moisten his eyeballs.

'What do you know about Roswell?'

'Officially or what I've seen in the *National Enquirer*?'

'Officially,' he said, giving me the deadeye again.

I shrugged, 'it was a weather balloon.'

'See?' he said triumphantly, 'the cover-up worked.'

Mom's voice drifted in from the kitchen, she asked us if we needed anything. Pop said wryly he needed another year of life, and Mom told him to stop being morbid. Mom continued to shuffle around out there for a while as Pop and I sat listening to Elvis.

'Is that *Now or Never*?' said Mom.

'Seems appropriate,' said Pop loudly.

Though I couldn't hear it, I knew Mom was muttering something under her breath. I heard her close the kitchen door and then go slowly upstairs.

'Make sure you and your sister look after her once I'm gone.'

'We will.'

'Okay,' said Pop, clapping his hands together as if he were about to start rubbing sticks together to start a fire.

'My buddy at OSU, at the Big Ear, his name's Jerry Ehman. He gave me a call back in August saying the telescope picked up something exciting. Now, just to clarify things, Big Ear operates on 1420 MHz. That frequency is solely used in the search for little green men, no one else can use it by law. About twenty years ago, a few academics and astrophysicists started getting into all that stuff and two of them at Cornell, Morrison and Cocconi, theorised if aliens wanted to talk, they might do so on that frequency.'

'Is it a special frequency?'

'It's the Hydrogen Line and as hydrogen is the most abundant element in the universe, they reasoned any technologically advanced society would know that was the number to dial. Are you following this?'

'I think so,' I said.

'Anyway, Jerry calls me and tells me they've picked up a doozy from somewhere near Sagittarius, and seeing as I'm dying and all, he thought I'd like to know.'

That puzzled me. I felt my brow wrinkle when he said it. Pop was a straight-up by-the-book research physicist his whole career. First with the military and then with industry. He never worked on anything 'out there' and often expressed disdain for the Space Programme. When Armstrong stepped on the Moon a decade before, he sneered and compared it to someone planting a tree in a car park. The question formed on my lips, but before I got a chance to ask him about it, he resumed his story.

'The universe is full of background noise, and Big Ear listens for anything out of the ordinary and gives a readout every night. Jerry is one of the guys who examines the readouts. The baseline, the bare minimum background noise, reads on the printout as 1. Most nights it's a whole lot of 1s, 2s and 3s. However, on the night of August 15th. Guess what it was?'

'I have no idea,' I said.

'I know, but will you humour me, for Christ's sake?'

'I don't know, 10 or something.'

He shook his head, evidently, I had not humoured him.

'6EQUJ5,' he said slowly and deliberately.

'Those six symbols were, as far as some people are concerned, a voice calling from the deepest, darkest wilderness. Now, I know a dummy like you won't know this, but that reading formed a normalised Gaussian curve. To put it in simple terms, during the 72 seconds of the recording the intensity rose for 36 seconds, peaked, and then descended for 36 seconds.'

He paused to gather his thoughts. I knew he was savouring the moment. There was a look of enormous satisfaction on his face.

'When Jerry saw the printout, he circled 6EQUJ5 and wrote Wow! In the margin.'

'Has he any idea of what it means?'

'Nope,' he said chuckling, 'they're trying to figure it out, but tell you what, I got an idea, and it's a good one.'

'What is it?'

He steepled his fingers and put them under his nose. They pushed the fleshy tip of his nose upwards, revealing the cavernous dark of his nostrils. I could hear him breathing heavily.

'I might leave the rest for the will,' he said.

'No way, man,' I said, 'you're not doing that.'

'Maybe I'll insert a clause saying you only get to find out if you have visited your mother every week for a year and that you've done a series of charitable acts for the community.'

'Fuck it,' I said, 'I'm going home, you can tell me later.'

I knew this mood. He'd tormented me with it all through my teens. He'd set me a riddle or some kind of teaser and then refuse to give me the answer. And then, eventually, when he did, it was so underwhelming I'd roll my eyes and leave the room in a funk. I knew this was one final shaggy dog story and while playing along was the right thing to do, I couldn't. Not that night, anyway.

I did ask why Jerry Ehman had called him.

'You were never into all that space stuff,' I said.

He appreciated my observation.

'In my last few days at Los Alamos, they threw me a little party,' he said. It wasn't much fun, but after I'd shook hands with all the brass, Richard Feynman and Enrico Fermi invited me to join them for a beer. Feynman was talking about a recent meteor shower he'd seen in the desert. He said it made him think about other worlds and whether we'd ever have contact with beings from other planets. Fermi dismissed the idea, saying the distances were too great and dangerous to navigate and how an alien species was more likely to destroy itself than master interstellar space travel. 'Just look at what we accomplished in 1945,' he said. 'I assure you; the human race will do the same.'

Pop paused for a sip of water.

'I couldn't accept this,' he continued. 'I'd heard rumours about the Roswell crash, though no one would confirm it. I told you they did a good job covering it up. So, for the rest of my career, I've been working in the shadows searching for little green men.'

I was completely bug-eyed, and Pop let out a proper laugh, one that shakes your whole body. I had to hand it to him, he knew how to pick a moment.

'Jerry and me and a few other guys have been looking at the skies for years.'

'Why?' I said, my voice barely a whisper over the impassioned strains of Elvis singing *Kentucky Rain*

'Because I'm a scientist and if ever there was a big question, whether we are alone in the universe is about the biggest I can think of.'

I drove home slowly. I felt displaced, as if I didn't belong in the world. I looked beyond the horizon to where the land merged with the sky, and there followed upwards to the scattered array of stars which filled the winter night. About a mile from home, I pulled over and got out and sat on the hood and meditated on the sky. A racing wind blew about my frame, but I ignored it. I don't know exactly how long I was there, but I recall coming to, or more precisely, re-entering the real world with a jolt. When I got home, I felt an unsettling mix of alertness and fatigue. I sat in the easy chair, tilted it back, and stared at the ceiling until I fell asleep.

Pop died on May 25th, exactly a year after *Star Wars'* release. The last movie we'd seen together was *Five Days from Home* in April. We hadn't spoken about aliens or anything in the final months and his last words to me were 'that was a good movie, thanks, son.'

Jim Blake, Pop's attorney, called me a week after the funeral and asked if I could drop by his office. I drove by that afternoon and Jim greeted me in his typically perfunctory manner and gave me an envelope. I took it, thanked him, and left. I sat in the car as the day's heat made one last push before the sun began to slip below the horizon. The envelope had my name on it and nothing more. Pop had left everything to Mom except for a few personal effects, which went to friends. It took a while, but I finally opened the envelope. The message was typical of Pop, concise and direct.

*If you want to know what I think 6EQUJ5 means give Jerry Ehman at the Big Ear a call. His number is on my desk.*

My first instinct was scepticism. Was this Pop's final practical joke? Would I call Jerry Ehman, and he'd ask me if I was crazy or something?

When I was about ten, Pop tricked me into calling The John Birch Society and asking if I could become a member. I thought I was calling to join The Boy Scouts. The man on the phone gave me a figurative pat on the head and sent me on my way. I decided, if this was Pop's last joke, playing along was the least I could do.

Jerry Ehman was happy to take my call. He was friendly and accommodating, and we spoke for some minutes about my father and his work.

'I never knew about this side of him,' I said.

'He was a great supporter of our work,' said Jerry, 'we're going to miss him.'

'Did you know he was fond of practical jokes?'

'No,' said Jerry, 'I only knew him as a dedicated and visionary scientist.'

'Seems he had a few secrets.'

'He was the first person I called after I'd seen the readout of August 15th,' said Jerry.

I still couldn't believe how Pop had kept his involvement with this research secret for years.

'I called your father the night of August 18th. The signal was broadcast on the 15th, but no one looked at the printout until the 18th.'

'Do you think it was a communication from aliens?'

'I think so.'

'What did my father think?'

'That's the thing,' said Jerry, his voice taking on a different tone, as if he were about to admit something embarrassing. I waited for him to continue.

'The signal was broadcast on the 15th of August, the day before Elvis died.'

I wasn't sure I was following.

'Your father thought the signal was a message telling Elvis to leave the building, in a manner of speaking.'

I laughed out loud and kept laughing. Jerry joined in and we shared a real belly-shaking guffaw. Good old Pop, he'd done it. It was a joke.

'Elvis was an alien. That's priceless. Looks like he got us both,' I said.

'Looks like it,' said Jerry.

'This is perfect,' I said, 'so typical of him. You gotta admit, he played me like a fiddle.'

Jerry was saying something, but I wasn't listening, I was too wrapped in the situation's absurdity.

Jerry's voice pulled me from my thoughts.

'There is one thing you need to know,' he said.

I couldn't place the tone of his voice. It had the grave earnestness of a doctor but mixed with the empathy of an elementary teacher.

'What is it?'

'There was another signal.'

'Really,' I said, 'when?'

'We picked it up the evening before your father died. It had the same intensity, a little different in specific detail but essentially the same and from the same region of space.'

I felt a sudden tightness in my chest, as if I were running out of air. I reached across the desk and pulled on the piece of paper I'd discarded at the start of our call. I read it slowly, twice.

'Was it 5GRWK4?'

A long, palpable silence followed, as if Jerry had vanished.

'Jerry, are you there?'

When I'd gone to find Jerry's number from Pop's desk, I noticed under Jerry's name, Pop had written 5GRWK4 several times. I thought it was a postcode or something and didn't pay it any attention, until now.

'Maybe you should come to the university sometime, we probably need to have a chat,' said Jerry.

I looked at the piece of paper and thought of my father and all the questions I wanted to ask him.

'I think you're right,' I said.

I hung up the phone and, after rubbing my face, stared at the wall for a long time.

# THE HEADLESS MEN OF THE NAHANNI VALLEY

It was past six and McPherson had been drinking since noon. A few of us had gathered to listen to him wax lyrical about the rainbow trout in Loch Corrib. 'The size of snowshoes,' he'd say, gesturing with his big, hard, leathery hands. None of us knew what size snowshoes were, but all of us knew there were no rainbow trout in The Corrib. I saw Norris take a notion to dispute McPherson's claim, so I frowned hard at him, and the rising objection sank and died somewhere in his throat.

'In Canada, the trout were the size of dogs,' said McPherson.

'Are we talking Rottweilers or Pomeranians?' said Benedict with casual ease before taking a long draught from his pint.

McPherson growled and grunted with wrinkled lip but proffered no illumination on the question. Of course, Benedict wasn't looking for an answer. I turned to Coxy, who was tending the bar, and asked for a pint. He looked tired. McPherson often had the effect of making people tired.

'He was here when I opened up,' said Coxy, 'standing in the cold like some stray.'

I nodded. I knew this story, just like I knew McPherson's stories and the stories of everyone else who told a tall tale in the bar.

'Marie probably kicked him out,' I said, 'or he's been out all night and came from somewhere else.'

Coxy shook his head.

'He looked like he'd washed when I let him in. He'd combed his hair, and it smelled of Brylcreem.'

'Brylcreem, really?'

'I'd know the smell of it anywhere.'

I shot a glance at the Canadian. His rust-coloured hair was sloppy and oily. It hung down on his forehead like streaks of terracotta ink blown across paper. He was drinking a customary Guinness, and his red beard was tinged with remnants of foam from the stout. He wiped his mouth unobtrusively and took a long drink. I thought he'd finish the entire pint in one swallow. He stopped halfway and put the glass down with a hard thud. He sat heavily in his chair but straightened after a moment. His eyes moved slowly across the company until they landed on mine.

'Sweeney, when did you get here?'

'Just arrived,' I said.

Norris looked at me accusingly. I furrowed my brow.

'Did I finish telling you about the time I explored the nightmarish interior of Nahanni Valley?

Finished, no, started, many times, I thought.

'You never quite finished the story. You saw a creature of some kind,' I said cheerfully.

'I did,' said McPherson as if he were resetting the narrative in his mind.

He paused a moment and cogitated on our exchange before finally accepting what I said was indeed true. He proceeded to locate the point where he'd left and declared he was now ready to continue his tale. I gestured to Coxy I'd have another and to put one on for McPherson. McPherson shot me a toothy smile and lifted his pint to salute my generosity. Coxy was nonplussed but set the pints to cook and McPherson resumed his tale, one begun several weeks before and, truthfully, begun when I'd first met him a decade earlier.

McPherson hails from Saskatchewan. He's rugged and hardy, and his face looks centuries older than his forty or so years. His skin is like the hard rind of a smoked pork belly, and his hands are gnarled as old bark. He's been through the wars, and like many soldiers, he's never entirely returned from the trenches.

'We set out from Fort Simpson along the Liard River,' he said with the zesty enterprise of a man about to tuck into a hearty meal.

'The river took us about thirty miles into the most ancient forest the world has to offer.'

Norris leaned into our orbit. I thought he was going to correct McPherson with some bollocks about Siberian forests. Over the years, I had to use the furrow of my brow more than once to let him know that any nonsense based on reason, logic or truth would not be tolerated. Norris, a retired taxman, once ruined a cracking joke I was in the process of telling by stating just after the punchline how the young lady's actions were contrary to the laws of physics. I told him if he ever did something like that again, we could conduct our own physics experiment by seeing how much force was required to put his head through the wall. As McPherson described the eerie silence of the Nahanni Forest, Norris was hovering a bit too close for my liking. I decided to keep one eye on him.

'There are places on the earth,' continued McPherson, his voice simultaneously giddy with story and gritty with mileage, 'no man was meant to traverse.'

'Such as the wilds of Borneo,' said Coxy, giving me a wink.

'To the vineyards of Bordeaux,' I added.

Coxy sniggered. I sipped my pint.

'For example,' said Coxy, by way of a coda.

McPherson's face screwed up. He looked as if he were trying to scratch an itch inside his head. Before long, the confusion ailing him passed. He then cleared his throat. It sounded like someone emptying a brown paper bag full of grease and broken glass.

'The Nahanni Valley is a place no man was meant to traverse.'

'Why so?' said Coxy, handing him a fresh pint.

McPherson turned his pint glass, so the harp faced towards him, and appeared to appreciate its elegance. He smiled and continued with his stilted tale.

'There is a race of creatures living in the forests. They're more ancient and terrifying than anything you might read about in the old mythologies.'

'That's something,' said Coxy.

'Are they like Bigfoot, or what's it called Sasquatch?' I inquired.

McPherson dismissed my comment with a contemptuous tut.

'Campfire stories for children,' spat the Canadian, 'what I'm talking about are devils so wild they can freeze a man's soul with a look.'

'Sounds like my ex-wife,' said Benedict.

There were hoots and laughs, even Norris managed a wry smile. McPherson's wife, Marie, was a formidable woman. Burly and well-able for him, she was his best friend and worst enemy all in one handsome body. She was from Laois and had four brothers. McPherson skirmished with each of them over the years. One time he managed to subdue Rosco and Seamus outside Rico's on Portlaoise Main Street during a wild Friday night. It was only when Daithí, the eldest brother, arrived and smacked him over the head with a hurl that order was restored. McPherson hit the deck and didn't wake up until the next day. It was all taken in jest and a year later, when baby Nuala was born, all was well, or as well as it can be for a family of drinkers who liked to beat the tar out of one another from time to time.

'Didn't a few lads go into the forest about a hundred years ago looking for gold?' said Coxy.

McPherson nodded.

'They never made it back alive.'

'Jaysus,' said Coxy, 'what happened?'

'The prospect of gold seduced many a man to go into that awful place. Those who made it out were lucky, some did not. When the bodies of those unfortunates were found, they all had one thing in common.'

'What was that?' said Coxy, on cue.

McPherson looked at each of us in turn before answering in a slow, resonant and sombre voice like a priest delivering the message of his sermon.

'They were all headless.'

'Good lord,' said Coxy, wiping a glass.

McPherson's voice took on a judicial tone. He lifted an index finger and shook it gently at us.

'To be clear,' he said, 'their heads were pulled off, not cut off, but pulled off the way you would pull the head off an old hen or the top off a bottle of beer.'

'With a bottle opener?' said Norris.

I felt my stomach drop. There was no point frowning at Norris now.

'What?' said McPherson.

Norris looked at McPherson with fixed, uncertain eyes. He'd clearly not been listening and stumbled into the story like a deer bounding from the trees onto a busy road. His comment jarred the flow of McPherson's story. McPherson stood up and took an unsteady step towards Norris.

'Easy now,' said Coxy, 'get back to your story.'

'What did you say?' pressed McPherson, ignoring Coxy.

Norris retreated, clutching his pint to his chest like a shield. I moved into the space between the two men. I wasn't as big as McPherson, but between myself and Coxy and Benedict, we could manage him. Just.

'I didn't say anything,' said Norris, his voice timid and barely audible.

'You've had a few,' said Coxy, reaching over the bar and tapping McPherson's arm, 'there's no need for words.'

McPherson turned on Coxy, he stared him down for about ten seconds before muttering an expletive and returning to his seat.

'You're fortunate,' he growled at Norris with sharp disdain, 'you're fortunate I'm not sober. Being sober tends to loosen my tongue.'

Norris slinked off into the shadows like some unpleasant, slimy nocturnal creature, and McPherson's dangerous mood subsided. Once he'd had a few mouthfuls from his pint, resumed his tale.

'We weren't looking for gold,' returned McPherson to no one in particular.

Something about the tone in his voice swept away the lingering aggression in his body. It became confessional, almost as if he were appealing to a higher power to deliver him from some burden. I had a palpable sense he was trying to communicate something which lay beyond the words available to him. The air in the bar thrilled with an energy which moved across my skin with the same unease as diving into deep water.

'There was a stretch of about ten miles where the river flowed through the living rock. On either side, there were cliffs as high as the eye could see. A fearsome darkness covered the water and all around the echoes of our paddles as they slapped the water beat a demented rhythm. We were quiet as monks during this part of the journey for fear they would hear our voices.'

'You mean the creatures?' I said.

'Not just the creatures,' said McPherson, 'the ancient ones.'

A pause followed. None of us were compelled to ask what McPherson meant by this, nor did the big man elaborate.

'Just as the light was fading, we reached our destination. We had precious little time to put up our tents and build a fire.'

'How many of you were there again?' asked Coxy.

'Four of us,' said McPherson grimly, 'we were young men, we thought we could do anything. One lad, name of Donaldson, had a great-uncle who'd been a trapper in Manitoba years before. He'd told us the stories of the Nahanni Valley and its headless men. He was a solemn drunk and what he told us was true. I saw it in his eyes.'

'Had Donaldson's uncle been there?'

'I don't know. He only told us the stories. One night he was about halfway through a bottle of rye when he started making pronouncements about how young men were soft and how men of his generation were the last hardy ones. We didn't take kindly to his words, but he didn't care. He said we were cowardly, but if we travelled into the Nahanni Valley and managed to return alive, he'd reconsider his position on the matter.'

'I'm not sure I'd be so brave,' I said with a chuckle, 'not sure I'd want my head popped off like a champagne cork.'

'We had no choice,' said McPherson.

The confessional tone returned to his voice.

'I'd had it all my life by then,' he continued.

I'd never heard him speak like this before. Coxy noticed it too. We shared a bemused look. McPherson resumed his tale. His eyes were becoming glazed, and his head was drooping in sudden jerks. I knew it wouldn't be long before we were throwing him into a taxi. After that, he'd be Marie's problem and most likely little Nuala's too.

'My father, my brothers and now Donaldson's uncle. The whole kit and kaboodle of them with their hard hands and thick necks and me with nothing.'

He stood up proudly, like a condemned man giving one final impassioned speech before the firing squad. He spoke in a booming voice that was somehow oddly quiet.

'It was me,' he said pushing back his greasy hair, 'I forced the others into that awful place. It was my vanity, my need to be respected by men I hardly knew, which took us into the depths of hell.'

'But you made it back,' I said, noticing my heart rate beginning to elevate.

McPherson made a startling noise somewhere between a laugh and a cry. He walked over to me and stood and placed his hands on my shoulders. They were heavy, like a stack of books. He looked awful. His eyes were red, and his pupils were wide. His face was grizzled and old, and a kind of unrelenting weariness reeked from every pore of his body. He looked me in the eye and then his head bowed. I thought he was about to cry. I certainly wasn't in the mood for a maudlin drunk. Thankfully, he lifted his head and looked at me once more. His eyes were dry. We remained locked in a gaze for a few seconds. I wanted to be free of him, but I could do nothing. He'd chosen me and was going to deliver his message to me and me only. A tiny smirk cracked along his lips and then vanished so quickly I was scare sure I'd seen it. He clapped his hands on my shoulders and let go and walked off towards the toilets.

It took a few moments before anyone could speak, and even then, no one knew what to say.

'Are you alright?' said Coxy.

I couldn't tell if I was. I know this seems mad, but somehow McPherson had shown me what happened on his trip into the Nahanni Valley. It wasn't a vision or telepathy, or any hocus-pocus like that. I can't really explain it, except I felt it. You can say what you like, but I know what happened.

We sat in silence, nursing pints for the next while. The sounds in the room became more intense. The ticking clock sounded like gears grinding and the shuffle of feet like nails on a chalkboard. Every atom in my body began to agitate and nothing could stop it.

'Where's McPherson?' said Benedict.

None of us had thought about him since his exit. Benedict's question appeared to dispel the strangeness within the room. The whole sensation was most peculiar. I felt like I was returning to reality from the tingly fog of a mushroom trip.

'Is he still in the jacks?' said Coxy.

'Maybe he left without being noticed,' suggested Benedict, 'he's done it plenty of times before.'

'Ben,' said Coxy, 'hold the fort, will you? I'll just check the jacks.'

Benedict nodded.

'I'll come with you,' I said.

I couldn't tell if Coxy was worried about finding McPherson dead for McPherson's sake or for his own. About a year before, an old duffer named Brady took a pint from the bar, sat in a booth and died. It was a double tragedy; he'd barely touched the pint.

'If we go in there,' said Coxy before opening the door to the jacks, 'and he's on the floor in a state, dead or alive, it goes no further than us. Let's protect his dignity, whatever we find.'

I nodded somberly.

McPherson wasn't on the floor. He was in a cubicle, sitting on the toilet. His pants were still around his waist and his head was tilted back on the wall. Coxy squeezed into the cramped space and put a finger up to the Canadian's neck.

'Is he alive?' I asked.

'I think so,' said Coxy, 'wait, there's a pulse.'

'Will I call a cab?'

Coxy stepped back and shook his head.

'Wait here,' he said.

An age passed before he came back. Being alone with McPherson gave me the creeps. I kept expecting his head to lift off the wall and fix me with that cold stare again. My mind raced with thoughts of being trapped in a tent as it was being ripped open and gigantic hands reaching for my head and twisting it until my eyes could see behind me. I could picture impossibly tall trees looming in the moonlit sky and the air full of voices trying to speak but being silenced before words came out. Before my head came off, I could see McPherson running towards the river. He was calling my name.

'Sweeney, Sweeney, Sweeney, what the fuck is the matter with you?'

It was Coxy. I must have looked a sight because his eyes had a hint of panic in them.

'Are you on something?'

'What?' I said, 'no, no, I'm … I don't know what's going on.'

'Okay,' said Coxy, pretending he hadn't momentarily stumbled into the Twilight Zone, 'once we've got McPherson sorted, you're going home. Got that?'

I nodded sheepishly.

Coxy went to the cubicle where McPherson slept and put an out-of-order sign on the door and closed it over.

'He's better off here. I'll deal with him once he wakes. I've told the lads I'm closing for the night.'

'I'd say they're delighted.'

'I don't care,' said Coxy.

'Want a hand getting rid of them?'

Coxy nodded.

Ten minutes later, we'd shuffled the few remaining off to The Oak down the road.

'Thanks for that, Sweeney,' said Coxy, ducking back inside.

'Will McPherson be alright?' I asked.

'He'll be grand, I'll make up a bed for him, make sure he gets home in the morning.'

'Give Marie a call,' I said.

Coxy nodded and disappeared inside. I waited while he closed the locks and slid the heavy bolt across the door before leaving to go home. I felt a sense of relief at each sound, that is, until they stopped.

Even though there were streaks of light hanging along the sky's furthest reaches, the darkness felt heavy. I didn't hurry, though. I needed to psyche myself up for the walk home. I dawdled in the reassuring presence of other souls who shared the street with me. Eventually, I reached the bridge and took a left into the uncertain terrain of the path home. The path ran parallel to the river's shimmering ribbon. In the overhanging willow branches, I was sure I saw things moving and in the surrounding countryside's never-ending blackness I felt as if I was being watched. From far off, strange noises jabbered incomprehensibly. They sounded as if they came from a world on the edges of this one. A little voice in my mind, piqued with curiosity, urged me to investigate.

I put my head down and moved into the hard dark. The elemental river, heavy and slow, like a creature whose age I couldn't even begin to fathom, spoke in sounds which rushed into my bones and stayed there. I could feel a thousand eyes watching me.

# IRVING EASTBROOK'S SNOW GLOBE

Everything about Joan and Irving Eastbrook was in the middle. They were in their mid-thirties; they were middle class, they had two children, and they lived in the middle of their street in a mid-terrace house in a gentrified part of the city. Irving's hair was beginning to thin, and he needed reading glasses. He drove a mid-range car, had a mid-level job in a medium-sized enterprise, and was going a little soft in the middle. Joan was every bit as average as her husband, though she fought much harder to disguise it. She was a plain woman, with medium-length brown hair, a pleasant but not especially warm smile and eyes of an indistinct shade somewhere between hazel and grey. Aware of her aesthetic limitations, she made the most of what she had by dressing well and accentuating her better features. Taking a view from afar, one would believe Joan and Irving Eastbrook had made a good life for themselves, and if you asked either of them, they would say they had little to complain about. Yet, lurking beneath the surface of their daily life, they retained the painfully middle-class aspirations of better jobs and a better home in a better area, bringing altogether a better standard of living.

There were obstacles, however. Irving didn't have the dynamic drive required to ascend to the next level and resisted Joan's gentle nudges. He worked in research for an engineering company and when the opportunity for advancement came along, he would ignore it, preferring the comfortable familiar to the uncertainty of new challenges. He would adopt a kind of disinterest, speaking with comic disdain about those who were chasing money and receiving higher levels of stress. At night, he would sometimes lie awake and swallow the tiny bubbles of resentment which grew in the creases of his heart. He knew who he was, and every so often he would remind himself with wonderful cognitive dissonance that by doing nothing to better his situation, he might just be doing the thing required to advance his case. It made sense to him, even if it didn't make sense. Joan, on the other hand, was much less given to fancy. She was a practical woman and was often hard on herself for letting envy distract her, not because she was particularly self-aware, but because it was a trait she loathed in others. She liked to browse expensive shops while imagining money wasn't an object.

Much of her shopping was online. She scoured the internet looking for bargains and discount codes. When she found something, she indulged in a private celebration. She knew Irving, whose name she felt was a throwback to a bygone age imbued with class and sophistication, would approve of her thrift, but she also knew it would embarrass them both to acknowledge it. The upshot of this was they never spoke about money, Irving paid the bills, the school fees and insurance. Joan paid for all matters concerning housekeeping, including the children's clothes and activities. Luxuries were few.

Their passion was reading. Joan tended towards book club books, sometimes she'd dip into a more literary book, but mostly she read the kind of book she could talk about casually at the supermarket or outside the school gate and appear smart, but not too smart. Irving read everything from comics to self-help books to Booker Prize winners to trivia. Joan was envious of his scope of interests, but she never showed it and would often scoff, in a playful way at what he read.

'Honestly, Irving, you're thirty-seven years of age, surely, it's time to put your *Tintin* comics away, or at the very least, give them to Oliver?'

Irving would smile and nod when Joan made this type of comment, but never reply with a comment of his own. They took pride in the fact they read at least one book a week. Even during the sleepless chaos when Oliver and Rose were infants, they managed it. Some nights Irving read aloud while Joan fed one or, sometimes both babies. It worked so fabulously they continued it once the storm of new parenthood passed. Though, like many things in their marriage, it had since dwindled to a faint ember.

Unsurprisingly, they were on a first-name basis with the local library staff. Genial as this relationship was on the surface, the library staff generally disliked them, or more precisely, disliked Joan. Joan would appear at the desk and with her wide, polite smile ask them to get the latest title by a particular author, and they would oblige and email her when it arrived. She would arrive at the library shortly thereafter and take the book with her. There was nothing about Joan or Irving's manner the staff disliked, for they were perfectly nice in the superficial way perfectly nice people are. It was, instead, their casual disregard for the books' welfare which caused opprobrium. Sometimes the books came back dogeared or with smudges from dirty fingertips. Once, a book was returned with a torn page. Irving apologised and offered to pay for it, saying he had sneezed while turning the page and the involuntary action caused the damage. Sue, the kindest librarian, decided not to charge Irving, but only because she felt sympathy for him. He was so mild and unassuming, and his glasses looked like they were from the budget range at Specsavers. His clothes were past their best, and something about him gave the impression of naivety. On the other hand, had Joan arrived with a book in similar condition, she would have fined her. She found Joan so obviously supercilious and felt a grinding rage when Joan would smile with her eyes. She had also heard from her colleagues how Joan Eastbrook was a bit of a busybody and given to the worst kind of gossip. Sue couldn't understand how Joan and Irving fit together and was especially confounded by their children, who were not only charming and lovely but so unlike their parents in affectation and temperament it seemed scarcely possible Joan and Irving had produced them.

One Sunday morning in March, Joan awoke and felt a stiffness in her neck. Irving was snoring beside her. She looked at the bulge of his belly and made a mental note to encourage him to do a little more walking. She turned her head slowly and the stiffness escalated into a sharp pain which made her yelp loudly. This surprised her, for she was never one to complain about personal discomfort. She'd trained herself through obdurate willpower to suffer in silence. This was all an effort to see if others noticed. Sometimes they did, especially Irving. Her cry woke him. He bolted upright and asked her what was wrong. As if a switch had been turned, Irving was out of bed and in the bathroom rummaging for liniment and Deep Heat and other such things. Finding nothing but an old tub of Vicks, he returned to his wife, feeling abashed.

'It's nothing, dear,' said Joan, 'I'll survive. We should get ready for church.'

'Are you sure?' insisted Irving.

'Quite sure,' replied Joan.

Irving looked at her with great concern, but with nothing to offer by way of comfort, he nodded and said he would get her a couple of painkillers. During church, Joan's stiff neck meant her scope of vision was limited to no more than 45 degrees on either side. She was left frustrated by being unable to look around and survey the sinful faces in the congregation and wonder what their sins were. Left to the equally limited scope of her imagination, she could only look at Reverend Deane and begrudge him his claim to having never sinned at all. After church, they visited a mid-range restaurant and ate a perfectly acceptable meal, which Joan found entirely unsatisfactory. The children enjoyed the colouring pencils and puzzles which were supplied for them by their enthusiastic waitress, and doodled while Joan and Irving finished their wine. Before they left the restaurant, Joan made the kids leave their handiwork behind. She didn't want any unnecessary clutter and told them so.

The next day, Joan was surprised to find a DPD driver at her door. She hadn't ordered anything and thought it odd Irving would order something without telling her. The delivery driver showed her the note and left the large cardboard box at her feet. She picked it up and discovered it was much lighter than she expected. It was addressed to Irving. She spent the rest of the day probing it in a state of perplexed curiosity.

By the time Irving got home, Joan was a knot of anticipation. She'd spent the afternoon making a list in her head of what could be in the box. It couldn't be something for a birthday, as weren't any forthcoming. It certainly wasn't an anniversary present. The sender's details on the box gave her no information.

Opening the front door, Irving enacted his usual ritual of announcing himself, taking off his coat and shoes before then moving to the living room where Joan would usually be. When he discovered she wasn't there, he lumbered into the kitchen.

'Ah, it arrived,' he said with delight.

Joan stood up, gave him a perfunctory kiss on the cheek and then stood back and watched as he opened the box using a key to slice the brown tape holding it together.

'Why didn't you open it?' he asked.

'It has your name on it.'

'I forgot to mention it to you this morning, sorry.'

'I was surprised when it arrived. Should I call the kids for the grand opening?'

'No need, it's not for them,' said Irving, giving her a wink.

He continued in a jocular tone: 'I'm sure you've been racking your brains all day wondering what it is.'

'Of course not,' said Joan, 'don't be silly. That's a silly thing to say.'

As Irving's hands delicately pried open the box, Joan watched with the excitement of a child on Christmas morning.

'Voila,' said Irving with a flourish. In his hands, he held a pillow. Joan was crestfallen. She looked at the pillow and when it didn't magically change into something wonderful, she turned to Irving.

'A pillow, how lovely

'There's two,' said Irving, taking the second from the box, 'they're ergonomic, I thought they might help with your neck.'

Joan's neck hadn't bothered her all day. Her hand reached to the back of her head and reflexively rubbed her neck.

'Is it still troubling you?'

'A little,' said Joan, 'thank you, Irving, thank you for being thoughtful.'

Already in her mind, she was ruminating through a litany of reasons to avoid using the pillow beyond the first few nights. She would use it for a couple of nights and then, claiming her neck was fine, would return to her former, undeniably comfortable pillow. She was confident Irving wouldn't even notice.

'Are they both for me?'

'I thought I'd get us one each. There was a good deal for two, so I thought why not,' said Irving, his face illuminated by the cheerful glow of someone who knew they'd got a bargain.

Joan smiled, all eyes and teeth, and searched in the cupboard for a paracetamol.

That night, she couldn't concentrate on her book. Irving was reading a weighty book about economics by some French author whose name she couldn't pronounce. He was certainly enjoying it, punctuating his reading with noises suggesting he was deep in thought. Joan's book, a standard potboiler, which she'd been enjoying, was now ruined by the presence of her new pillow. She moved it around to get comfortable, but it was too firm for her. Every ten minutes or so, Irving would mention how he felt more comfortable now his neck was supported properly. Joan would agree and turn her back and read the same paragraph for the fifth time. Eventually, she turned off her bedside lamp, leaving Irving to his French economist, and fell into a shallow sleep which then became the best night's sleep of her life.

She awoke to thick bars of honeyed light and immediately felt a lightness in her body and mind. Ordinarily, she would have reached for her phone, but the feeling of comfortable completeness was all-encompassing and filled her with a radiance which, had she been a little broader in her imaginative scope, she might have thought she was Goldilocks or Sleeping Beauty. The steady rise and fall of Irving's paunch beside her was no longer an ugly thing. She reached across to touch it. For a moment, she entertained a naughty thought, but as it was a Tuesday and Irving had work and the kids needed to be woken up for school, she let it go, feeling instead the weekend was a more appropriate time for such things. She stretched in the deeply satisfying, full-bodied way a dog does. Only when she got out of bed and instinctively fluffed her pillow did she pause and consider if the pillow had anything to do with her perfect, dreamless night of undisturbed sleep.

Half an hour later, Irving, showered and dressed, came down to the kitchen. Joan looked at him and her mouth dropped open a little. His hair was combed neatly and not in the haphazard way of his more usual custom. His clothes were ironed, and he wore a new shirt. She felt her nose wrinkle, he was wearing aftershave. The good aftershave her sister gave him for Christmas.

'You smell nice.'

'I do?'

Joan moved close to him and enjoyed the rich olfactory aroma of cedar and citruses, revealing the long-buried masculinity of her husband in a great wave of delicious sex appeal.

'Did you sleep well?' she asked, flashing her eyelashes.

'Like a stone, you know, I may have had the best night's sleep of my life.'

Joan was rapt. Amorous feelings for Irving began to rise within her. She had a notion to throw her arms around him, but he moved to the coffee machine and the thread of her interest snapped.

'Where did you get the pillows?' she asked.

'They came from Germany, had them shipped overnight, the company guarantees ...'

'Guarantees what?'

'The best sleep of your life or double your money back,' said Irving, utterly bemused.

'You know,' he continued, 'I always thought such claims were gimmicks, but it looks like this company actually fulfilled its promise.'

'Wow,' said Joan.

Soon after, she accompanied Irving to the door, and they shared a proper goodbye kiss. It was like something out of a Nora Roberts story. As Irving walked to his car, the kids in tow, Joan stood in the doorway and waved them off and basked in the envious glances she could sense from her neighbours. She could see Mrs Hutchinson and Mrs Delaney and Mrs Linwood huddled like conspirators. After Irving's car turned the corner, she waited for a few moments to see if any of her neighbours might approach her to engage in casual conversation. It was rare enough they did anything like that. Joan put it down to the fact they were older and had little in common with her. She was about to go back inside when Mrs Hutchison called her. Joan turned and smiled at her neighbour. Her immediate thoughts were about Mrs Hutchinson's rumoured drinking problem and the obvious fact she carried too much weight.

'Sorry to bother you, Joan, but I was wondering if you'd seen Zippy?'

Zippy was the Hutchison's equally corpulent cat. Sometimes he would flop over the wall and sun himself in Joan's back garden, though Joan noted she'd not seen him in a few days.

'No,' said Joan, 'I haven't.'

'Oh,' said Mrs Hutchison, 'I know he likes to visit your garden.'

Mrs Hutchison looked visibly distressed but Joan, realising she had no interest in comforting her neighbour, said she was sure the cat would turn up sooner or later and went inside.

That night, a noise prompted Joan to get out of bed and make her way to the back garden. She could hear the soft moaning of an animal in need of help. She stepped into the cold spring night and onto the grass and then towards the shed which lay at the bottom of the garden. The noise was coming from inside, and when she opened the stout wooden door, Zippy sprang out and disappeared up the wall and into the next garden. She returned to bed and then woke up. It was morning and Irving was already up, pottering around the room.

'I've had the strangest dream,' said Joan in a faraway voice.

She got up with purpose, threw on her dressing gown, and bounded down the stairs. Irving watched her go, shook his head and once he'd located his cufflinks, he toddled down the stairs after her. The children were awake and getting dressed. He told them, in his gentle way, to get a move on.

Downstairs, Joan was in the garden. Irving came into the kitchen and moved to the window, where he could see her opening the shed. He flicked the switch on the coffee machine when, without warning, a greyish-brown blur moved with great speed from the shed and up the wall and into their neighbour's garden. A few moments later, Joan returned inside. She had a curious look on her face, as if she were trying to solve a complex equation in her head.

'What were you doing?' asked Irving.

'Irving,' said Joan slowly, 'if I were to tell you something odd, you wouldn't think I was odd, would you?

'That depends on what it was you said,' returned Irving, 'but probably not, no.'

Joan took a moment to compose herself before speaking, as if she were about to do a piece of workshop theatre.

'Yesterday Mrs Hutchison asked me if I'd seen Zippy,' she began.

Irving's brow arched. Joan glanced to her left and continued.

'She told me he was missing. I said I hadn't seen him but last night, or more precisely, this morning I dreamt Zippy was in our shed and when I checked just now, he was. Isn't that strange, I mean, how a dream communicated it to me?'

Irving took a sip of his coffee. The kids came into the kitchen and began to noisily gather bowls and cereal and toast and orange juice. Joan was too distracted to tell them to be quiet. Irving walked over to the window and looked down the garden. He took great pleasure in springtime. The world was greening again, and he lost himself in such thoughts until Joan repeated her question. He drank some more coffee and turned towards her.

'It's not strange at all,' he said, 'there's a perfectly logical reason for it.'

Joan pushed her lower lip into a pout and narrowed her eyes.

'Yes,' continued Irving, 'I suspect you saw the cat enter the shed yesterday or so. I know the door was slightly ajar and, I imagine the cat went inside, fell asleep, and got locked in. When Mrs Hutchison asked you about the cat, it probably triggered something in your subconscious, and you dreamed about it. There is a proven link between dreams and the subconscious.'

Joan nodded, what Irving said was plausible. That is, until it happened again.

This time, her dream was a little more sinister than a trapped tabby. The previous winter there'd been a spate of burglaries in the neighbourhood and every house along the street, alarmed or not, was targeted. The security of each house held firm, but a few things were stolen, like bikes chained up outside and garden equipment left in unlocked sheds. The law had been perfectly useless, but since no house got broken into, the neighbourhood counted itself lucky.

Joan awoke on the Wednesday morning and immediately told Irving about her dream. She related how during her dream she found herself in what was commonly known as The Big House. The Big House was a large, detached house with a high wall. It was owned by Mr and Mrs Prescott. He was a retired accountant, though his wife still worked, volunteering at the church. Some years before, Joan and Irving had been at a church-related party in The Big House. Joan remarked to her husband how opulent and stylish the place was. Irving nodded along to her words, but the limited of his interest extended only to the finger sandwiches and vol-au-vents and abundant and delicious wine. Now, after her dream, she told Irving the details she recognised and how she was sure it was going to be burgled that night. Irving wanted to dismiss his wife's concern, but her manner was so earnest, he had to entertain her belief.

'If you're right,' he said, 'what do you propose we do about it?'

Joan mused for a moment before eventually deciding she would make a phone call to the police. She told Irving she would simply say she saw some suspicious-looking characters snooping around The Big House and leave it at that.

Two days later, when Irving learned about the foiled burglary at The Big House, he was forced to take Joan's claims seriously on all dream-related revelations. Over the next month, Joan dreamed most nights about her neighbours and their lives. She would tell her husband about how the various families along the street were struggling to pay bills or contending with a relative who was unwell or, on a more positive note, were planning trips abroad and whatnot.

'It's very exciting,' said Joan one morning after giving Irving salacious gossip regarding Mr Delaney's business trips.

'He's having an affair, Irving. I saw it. I mean, I saw him and his mistress, I don't mean I saw them, you know, at it.'

Irving nodded. Initially, he'd found her stories engaging, even compelling, but now they were intrusive, and he feared they were beginning to consume the happiness of their home. He'd noticed a definite change in Joan's manner. It was like something was peeling off her surface layer, only to reveal something un-pleasant underneath.

'I can't believe the things people do,' said Joan.

'In the privacy of their own homes,' said Irving.

'Don't be so self-righteous, Irving, I always knew moralising ran in your family, but I don't need the lecture.'

'What's wrong with you?'

'Nothing,' said Joan, a thin veneer of petulance in her voice.

'You need to concentrate on yourself, Joan, you know what I mean?'

She stood up, adopting a confrontational pose.

'No, Irving, what do you mean?'

Irving took a moment to articulate his thoughts.

'Perhaps you should go back to using your old pillow and reading before bed instead of looking at your phone,' he suggested.

Joan ignored him and sat back down and began to turn the pages of her magazine.

'If nothing else, it would be a worthwhile scientific inquiry,' he intoned, 'your dreams coincide with the pillow's arrival, I wonder if the two are correlated and, if they are, what should be done about it.'

He added: 'it might improve your mood too.'

'Don't be stupid, Irving, it's a coincidence, I've never heard such a stupid thing, you and your science. Science isn't the answer to everything,' said Joan, without looking up from her magazine.

Irving motioned to say something back to her, but seeing her immovable and filled with what he took for disdain, he thought the better of it and left for work. Nothing more was said about the pillow.

Ever the student of behavioural science, it occurred to Irving the best subjects for any study of the complexities of personality were those who were utterly unaware they were participating. On the day Joan refused to change her pillow, Irving had swapped it with his own. He took the pillowcases from the pillows and switched them. He reasoned if Joan's pillow were somehow the cause of her dreams, then they would stop. What perplexed him most was the fact that his pillow, identical in every way, had not caused him to have strange dreams. Instead, he'd slept blissfully well. This thought was swirling in his mind as he put his head down on Joan's pillow.

He didn't sleep well. Joan was restless the entire night. She was asleep but moved in a perpetual state of discomfort as if she were sleeping in a hot climate on a humid night. He woke feeling tired but shrugged it off with a cold shower. Joan was subdued that morning and while sipping her tea at breakfast reminded him the annual PTA meeting at the school was that evening, and she expected him to attend.

'I've gone for the last two years; you should go this year.'

'OK,' said Irving without complaint, 'I'll leave work early. Did you sleep well?'

'Yes, you?'

'Yes, perfectly.'

When Irving and the kids were gone, Joan rushed straight up-stairs and replaced her pillow. She knew what Irving had done. It wasn't only the dreams she missed; it was the dreams between the dreams, which had begun about ten days before. In these dreams, she had everything she wanted, a perfect life with every-thing as it should be and if Irving wasn't going to give her that in the real world, she was damned if he was going to steal it from her imagination.

When Irving came home that evening, he called the kids to the family room and gave glowing reports about how their teachers thought the world of them. Joan's enmity subsided. She saw through Irving's ploy and would wait. For now, she basked in the lovely words he spoke and complemented Oliver and Rose about how smart and polite and wonderful they were. The kids lapped up the praise like a cat at a bowl of rich cream. A short time later, the kids had returned to their rooms and Joan and Irving were sitting in the living room. Irving was watching a documentary on TV and Joan was scrolling through her phone.

'I met Mrs Delaney at the shops this afternoon,' said Joan.

Irving looked over at her.

'I felt obliged to tell her that her husband is having an affair.'

'Did you?'

'No,' said Joan with a chuckle, 'I thought it best to say nothing.'

'Besides,' said Irving, 'you have no proof.'

Joan scratched her nails along the chair's upholstery. Irving baulked at the sound.

'Don't do that, you know I hate it.'

'Why did you switch the pillows?'

Irving turned off the TV, rubbed his eyes and sat back in his chair.

'Did you think I wouldn't notice?'

Irving got up and walked into the kitchen. At the sink, he got a glass of water.

'What gave you the right to do that, Irving?' said Joan, following him.

Irving drank the water and stared at her implacably.

Joan pointed to the walls, the cabinets, and the windows.

'You won't even let me have a nice home; look at this place, when was it last painted? I don't understand you. Everyone else on this street has a nice home, but not us, it's no wonder our only visitor is a fat cat who gets stuck in our shed.'

'Your sister visits.'

'Yes, and every time she comes over, I am mortified by the disgusting hovel of our home.'

Irving calmly put the glass on the draining board and moved towards his wife.

'Maybe,' he said, 'maybe if you weren't such a busybody, maybe if you were a little less concerned with things and more with people, we'd have visitors and friends and not have neighbours hurry past our door in case they get stuck in a conversation with you.'

'Irving, you can't speak to me like that.'

'I just did,' said Irving, leaving the room.

'Where are you going?' demanded Joan.

'I'm going to bed,' said Irving, closing the door with a firm thud.

As Irving made his way upstairs, a terrible thought occurred to Joan, and she scrambled after him. By the time she was halfway up the stairs, he was already in their bedroom and had locked the door. She pulled hard on the handle, but it only rattled, mocking her effort. When she began to bang on the door and call Irving's name, the children emerged from their rooms and asked what was wrong. Joan ignored them and a moment later the bedroom door opened with a click and Irving called for them all to come in. The kids ran into their parents' bedroom in eager anticipation. Joan followed with the reticent circumspection of someone examining a crime scene. As she came into the room, she saw Irving standing in a storm of swirling feathers, holding a ripped pillow. He picked up the other pillow and tore it open like he was eviscerating an animal, and began to shower the room with down feathers. Joan's eyes, wide and glassy, just stared and stared.

'I was thinking just now,' said Irving, a wry smile cracking across his face, 'what it would be like to live inside a snow globe.'

The kids laughed and began to bounce around in the falling feathers.

Irving continued: 'I guess it would be like this, eh kids?'

Irving and the children were laughing with unbound glee, and they danced around the room in a flurry of fun and excitement, while Joan stood there frozen stiff. As he passed the door, pursuing the kids, Irving grabbed her hand and pulled her towards him.

'You really should lighten up,' he said.

# YOURS EVER, ERICA

There were only ever two cases I worked on in my thirty-three years as a detective which threw me in a way I couldn't rationalise. The work was often hard, but it made sense in the way things in the real world do, except for those two times. God knows I saw some terrible things in my time. I witnessed every kind of depravity and cruelty you can imagine but also some things you can't, which is lucky for you, believe me. I was never much of a writer and found it hard to describe these things back then except as facts in prosaic reports. Sometimes there was a surreal, even comic, quality to the things I saw, like the time I was the first responder on the scene of a gangland shooting and didn't realise there was brain matter on my shoe until I got home and found the dog sniffing with unusual excitement around my feet. I remember turning the shoe and seeing a pink jelly on its edge and thinking, *Jesus, that's a piece of someone's brain.*

Yes, I'd seen it all, as they say and after the first few times, I became inured to the testimony of violence which went with the territory of my job. My colleagues were grudgingly impressed by my ability to detach and referred to me mockingly as *The Iceman*, though never to my face. I hated the name. *What's your secret? they'd ask, how can you see a child beaten half to death and treat it like you're changing a fucking lightbulb?* Don't you feel things? Despite what they thought, I wasn't a cold person, I could simply compartmentalise much better than most of my colleagues, shut out the bad stuff and accept it as part of the job.

I put it down to the Jesuits. At six, I'd been carted off to boarding school and learned crying after the lights were extinguished was something you did only once. The twelve years I spent there must have done something to my feelings because I did have ice in my veins. Nothing fazed me, not when Mick Liston or *The Shark* as he was known in the criminal underworld cornered me on a stakeout and hung me on a coat hook by the collar, laughing maniacally as I struggled to free myself. Liston, a truly bad egg, then pushed a gun into my face and told me he'd enjoy chopping me up and feeding me to the pigs. *Would that be cannibalism*? He'd joked, showing the jagged, dirty teeth which gave him his nickname. *Would it piggy*? he sneered and twisted the gun into my face. Liston was a sadist and had no intention of killing me quickly, and I knew it. He expected me to plead for my life, to beg him not to leave my children without their father, typical stuff like that. I was to submit completely to his will, and only when he had broken me would he deliver the coup de grace. I knew what to do, and staying calm was the key. When he repeated the question, I told him the wall separating my back garden from my neighbour's offered no privacy. I said it as matter-of-factly as possible. Liston was completely thrown by the comment. He looked at me as if the world had become suddenly strange. It was a risk on my part, for sure, but it meant he didn't start torturing me, for torture is mechanical and requires a clear mind.

Instead, he began to beat me. I was discovered about an hour later and when I came around two days later, despite being barely able to speak, I related my experience. No one could figure out why Liston hadn't killed me, but I knew, I'd seen it in his eyes while he lashed out desperately, flailing at my head and body with the crazed panic of someone caught in a falling dream. Three months later, when I returned to work, I was reading an old case file when the phone on my desk rang. I put it to my ear and heard the familiar voice of an informant I used from time to time telling me Liston was dead, and his body would never be found. It was the last time I heard mention of Mick Liston's name, and also the last time I heard from the informant.

Regardless of what the job brought, when I got home and felt the comfort of familiar things, I was able to step away from everything as if emerging into light after being underground. I had a wife and two kids and the aforementioned dog. All of us were young then and while, thankfully, the four humans are still alive, the dog is long gone. My wife and I are getting on a bit now. I'm still at home. I have a new dog and my son and daughter live nearby. I see them regularly. About a decade ago, when she was in her late fifties, my wife began to show the first signs of the dementia which would finally take her from the family home and put her into residential care. I didn't want it to happen, but I couldn't look after her, even with daily home help. The beating Mick Liston gave me had left me with permanent damage to my left lung and as I aged, I found anything involving physical effort like lifting, difficult. I'd also hurt my back in a fall down a flight of stairs while chasing a suspect. I know they look after her well and I see her every day. I can't tell if she knows who I am, but sometimes when she sees me her eyes light up for a moment, and she smiles like the first time I saw her on the bus from Dublin to Galway in 1977.

I was fresh out of Templemore and taking a few days off before starting my beat on the streets, I'd headed west to see a friend who was studying law at the university there. I was walking down the aisle, heading towards the back, when our eyes met. She smiled in a way which made my entire body tingle with electricity. I had no clue about women, the Jesuits had impressed upon me ideas such about women as to make me apprehensive, but this smile momentarily lifted whatever sense of shame I felt and after taking my seat I could think of nothing else. For over an hour as we passed out of Dublin through the city hinterland and into Kildare and Westmeath I was beguiled and bound by a desire to talk to her. Like the poet looking down the roads diverging in a yellow wood, I lingered a long time before taking the road less travelled. I decided at the least I'd have a story to tell my friend once I got to Galway. I was beginning to think of ways I could embellish the tale to make the girl on the bus even more beautiful, even more desirable when I found myself standing at her seat. Luckily, the seat beside her was unoccupied. I'd no idea how to go about chatting her up but as if I were watching a movie, I heard myself ask her if I could sit down and when she said yes, I hit reality so hard I almost scurried back to my seat like a crab hiding from a predator. She told me her name and I told her mine and the rest, as they say, is history.

I didn't see as much of my university friend that weekend, but he turned it into a good anecdote at my wedding. He's dead now, but for years after, when we'd meet socially, he'd refer to the weekend without fail. A few years later, the kids arrived, and life settled into a comfortable routine. I'm a creature of habit, always have been. I put much of it down to the sense of order and discipline drilled into me at school. It always seems to go back to school with me. School was the source of my earliest traumas. I sometimes wonder if it's somehow all related, like the hidden parts of a watch. I can't seem to figure it out, and when I think I have solved the mystery, the thought tends to run away from my mind. I suppose that's why I'm setting this down. If I can't figure it out, then perhaps someone reading this can. There is also the possibility there's nothing to figure out, there were many cases in my career that simply happened and didn't require an explanation. This is the curse of being ordered and matter of fact. I need to make sense of things whereas my wife, on the other hand, is anything but disciplined, or was. Sadly, her life as it is now runs with the clockwork precision of the German rail system, which she would hate; however, I am comforted somewhat by the truth that she's completely oblivious to her surroundings.

When she was in good health, she was the purest embodiment of a free spirit. Easy-going and creative and messy. What I remember most from when the kids were young was coming home, usually after a hard day, to find the three of them sitting in the living room or kitchen with glue and lollipop sticks or paper and paint. They would often be so absorbed in whatever they were doing, they wouldn't notice me. I would stand at the door, sometimes leaning on the jamb, and watch them swim in the world of their imaginations. Maybe because there wasn't a creative bone in my body, I found the process of art both fascinating and incomprehensible. I suppose the act of putting down these words is a form of art since it tells a story, but it's nothing like the world of pure imagination that my wife and kids lived and breathed all those years ago. I often felt like I was trespassing into their space, or maybe not trespassing as much as wandering into areas I didn't understand because I was always welcome. I guess the word tourist sums it up best. Regardless of whatever label I attached to it, I was the outsider, though it certainly had its compensations. Aside from the routine and the reassurance, I would sometimes stumble upon what was literally another world.

When my daughter was about five, she had an imaginary friend named Erica. For some reason, I was the one invited into this relationship, though I thought my wife was a more natural fit. I played along with the tea parties and how we would place an empty chair at the dinner table. It was harmless and a lot of fun until one evening my daughter said Erica wanted me to find her. I asked her what she meant by this, and she told me Erica was in the ground because a bad man had put her there. Something about my daughter's tone of voice chilled me to the core, as if the coldest winter wind had rushed through me. I asked her where Erica was, and she named a local school. I immediately recalled the building which housed the school had, until about fifteen years before, been a reformatory and how awful things had been done there. Sadly, in Ireland in the 1980s, The Church could act with impunity. I was a little confused, though, as it had been a boys' reformatory. My daughter looked into my eyes in a way which in any other moment would be endearing, but in this moment, was disconcerting, even frightening. She said because I was a policeman, I could find the bad man and put him in jail. I told my daughter I'd try my best, and she grew content. For a couple of days, my head spun with a variety of thoughts about whether to take her seriously. Except she named a place I knew; I could have put it down to her imagination. Eventually, I decided to do a little casual investigating with the expectation of finding nothing. Then I'd be able to tell my daughter the police didn't know anything, and that would be the end of it.

Within an hour of putting my mind to the task, I'd discovered an Erica who'd gone missing twenty-four years before from a nearby park and that she had been five years old and after a brief search, her disappearance had been noted in a file and boxed away with several similar files. I noted, Erica, whose surname was O'Connor, was the youngest of three children. Her childhood was marked by poverty and indifference, so it wasn't surprising to me that whoever was charged with finding her had not devoted a lot of time to it. It was often a matter of manpower, there simply weren't enough people to put in the work to find out things and follow leads, which usually led to dead ends. In some cases, it was down to diminishing returns. If a kid from a more affluent community went missing, especially if it came with the clout of a local politician, then it was all hands to the pump. I was part of a few circuses in my time. There would almost always be an answer sooner rather than later. Sometimes the kid came home, sometimes we'd find them in a ditch, sometimes worse, but rarely was it unsolved. The truth was, if the kid was poor, it was easier to say they ran away, even when we knew they hadn't.

We found Erica's body on an overcast and cold November morning. It had taken months to get a search warrant, after all. I had to satisfy myself first there was merit in pursuing the case, and then convince my superiors before any talk of going to a judge. In the months before we found her, the atmosphere at home became strange, not so much with my wife and kids, but with myself. I felt a presence in the house. I can't describe it in any other way. It existed in the dark corners of every room and was always there when I awoke. My daughter no longer spoke of Erica, and I grappled with what that meant before coming to the realisation Erica had made herself known to my daughter to get my attention. Now she'd latched on to me. I didn't know why. I only knew she inhabited the shadow within my shadow.

I put some time into it and with the help of a man I knew who worked with local welfare groups. He was sympathetic to the case, despite the timeline meaning a prosecution would be unlikely. It was taxing work. We asked a lot of people a lot of hard questions but in due course, we found out Erica had been seen in the company of a man who'd been known at the time to the local police and known to have certain unwholesome proclivities concerning children. He'd been a caretaker in the school my daughter had mentioned. The link was a little tenuous for my boss, but he took it to a judge, and we got our warrant. It took a week of searching, but we found human bones. I wasn't there when they were taken from the ground, but according to those who were, it began to rain and didn't let up until every last piece of her was removed from the wet clay. The day the body went to the State Pathologist, I was sitting down to dinner when my daughter, sitting to my left, put her hand on mine and told me Erica had said thank you. I smiled at her, but in doing so, I must have betrayed a buried emotion because my wife asked me what was wrong. I didn't respond, and later she told me I looked scared. I don't know why, because I wasn't scared, I was a little unnerved by the strangeness of how justice had been served, but it was nothing I couldn't handle. The real strangeness came a few days later when the Chief Inspector called me into his office, initially to congratulate me on closing the book on Erica's disappearance, but also to inform me she'd probably been murdered. Her hyoid bone had been fractured, which pointed towards strangulation.

'It's been forty years,' I said, 'her killer is probably dead.'

His face had a far-away look for a moment, and he turned his head to the right as if someone had called his name. I looked to where he was looking and standing there was a little girl with short black hair wearing a plum-coloured school uniform. Her expression was impassive, and she fidgeted with her hands. The CI was speaking, but I didn't hear him until he called my name loudly and with that, the girl disappeared right before my eyes as if someone had turned off a projector.

'According to the pathologist,' continued the CI, 'the bones have been in the ground no more than ten years.'

'Ten years, I don't understand,' I said.

'We obviously don't have the child who disappeared forty years ago, except ...'

'Except what?'

'There was a bracelet on the body which was inscribed with the child's name and date of birth.'

'What do you want me to do?' I said, my voice remote, like an echo.

'I don't know.'

Whatever truth lay within the mystery it wasn't revealed to me, certainly not at that time and if, as you'll read in these pages, it was revealed, I am at a loss to make sense of it. Despite the best efforts of those involved, the child's identity was never discovered. I was put on to something else and told not to pursue what was essentially trying to find a needle in a haystack. When I argued it was important to find the truth, my boss told me it was a waste of time. I pushed back, and he told me it was my final warning, and the conversation would go no further. It bothered me, but after a while, it drifted away from the front of my mind and into the folded layers of my subconscious. As the years passed, its call became fainter like the echo of an echo, until all that remained was a whisper in the wind or a flicker in the distant shadows at the bottom of a street at dusk. It eventually became quiet, or more accurately, dormant. I hadn't thought about Erica for long time, almost thirty years in fact, and was not far from retirement when whatever peace had evolved in the intervening years was now shattered in a way which has resonated ever since.

It was late afternoon one Friday in mid-May, and I was looking forward to finishing up and going home. My daughter and her husband were at a wedding and my three-year-old grandson was staying with us for the weekend, and I was excited to spend time with him. The sharp light had gone from the day and a hue of gold hung in the room as I stared vacantly out the window, lost in thoughts I can't recall. I was rudely returned to reality by the impatient buzzing of my mobile phone. It was one of my colleagues, and he sounded a little hurried, as if he was trying to relay as much information as he could in a limited time. I told him to relax, that he wasn't making sense, and to say clearly what he had babbled into my ear when I'd answered the phone. I blew out my cheeks as I listened to him describe what had happened, and, with a sinking heart, came to the dismaying realisation that spending time with my grandson might be delayed. I told my colleague I was on the way and left immediately. On the way, I called my wife and spoke for a few seconds to my grandson, telling him I'd see him soon.

When I got to the Gresham Hotel on O'Connell Street, the city was already bustling with early evening energy. I'd parked around the corner on Cathedral Street and walked briskly to the hotel. My colleague, a tall, thin, and ambitious junior detective who I knew was gunning for my job when I stood down, was waiting for me. He greeted me perfunctorily and hurried me through the lobby and to a lift, which we took to the third floor. As we rode the lift, he explained once more what he'd told me on the phone.

'Deceased male, about your age, maybe a little older, hard to say exactly.'

'Thanks,' I said sardonically.

'As I said, old guy, tied up, with a plastic bag over his head, hence the difficulty with his age.'

'I know, you told me that, I understand. It was the other stuff which made no sense.'

'You can see for yourself, if you don't believe me.'

The lift stopped and sank into its resting position.

'The body hasn't been touched,' said my colleague as the doors rolled open, ending with a resonant thunk.

He stepped out and turned right without a further word. I followed him. I had no particular interest in speaking with him.

When we got to the room, which was at the back of the hotel, facing into a small interior courtyard, he stood back, took out his mobile phone and leaned against the wall.

The door to the room had been taken off the hinges and stood propped up beside the frame. Two large men in black with steely expressions who I presumed were hotel security stood outside the room, and in front of them stood the hotel manager. As I approached, he moved towards me and greeted me with a kind of frantic enthusiasm, as if I were rescuing him from something dreadful. He explained the situation and I told him I'd been briefed by my colleague. I walked to the door and asked the security to step aside. They both looked at me with a cold, functional hardness before stepping aside.

I entered the room and, rounding the bathroom wall, I saw the dead man. He was as described. I did a cursory examination before focusing on the man and in particular his head. The plastic bag hadn't been tied like his hands and feet but had been pulled tightly over his head. I lifted it off and as I did the man's mouth opened and his tongue protruded, giving me a start. I walked to the window and pulled back the blackout curtain. I pulled out a latex glove and put it on and lifted the window handle and pushed it. It moved about four inches, enough to let in some air, but not enough for someone to get out, or in.

I called my colleague into the room. He came in with the manager following him like a terrier.

'A call was placed to the reception desk at 5 pm saying the occupant was leaving the room and would like it cleaned before they returned later in the evening,' said my colleague.

The hotel manager nodded.

'When the cleaner got to the room, she used her pass key to gain admittance, but when she pushed the door, it was stuck. She tried a couple more times before calling the desk, who then sent maintenance to take a look. The maintenance worker eventually had no other option but to take the door from its hinges.'

'A door stopper had been placed under the door,' said the manager, his voice breathy and jittery with nerves.

I returned to the window and looked around once more. I looked at the ceiling and then walked slowly to the bathroom.

'The door is the only way in or out,' said the manager.

I nodded and told him he could leave, and we'd have the body removed, and the scene processed as quickly as possible. He thanked us, but didn't seem in the least reassured. He told us the security men would stay until the room was cleared. I told him it was fine. Before he left, he added another detail. The dead man had asked specifically for a room hidden away in the hotel's interior, away from the street. The manager finished by telling us that while this was not an unusual request, the man had been vehement in ensuring it was fulfilled.

'What do you think?' asked my colleague once the manager had gone.

'I have no idea, the fact he asked for this room is interesting.'

'In what way?'

'I don't know yet.'

'The staff who discovered him thought it was a suicide.'

'We can't rule it out.'

My colleague let out a short laugh. I ignored him.

'Until we can prove this man was killed by someone else, we have no choice but to believe he did it to himself.'

'If you're right, it's an impressive trick.'

'Impressive isn't the word I'd use,' I said.

I leaned in close to the dead man and reached into his jacket pocket. I found nothing and moved to his trouser pockets.

'He checked in yesterday evening,' said my colleague, 'his name is, or was, David Scott.'

'I doubt that's his real name, but do the usual check. Someone probably knows this man.'

'What makes you think it's a false name?' asked my colleague, a hint of disdain in his voice.

'He didn't bring a bag.'

Aside from the hotel fixtures, the room was bare. There were no clothes hanging in the closet or toiletries in the bathroom. It crossed my mind how people who committed suicide in hotels often came without travel essentials, but I knew this wasn't a suicide, despite what I'd said to my colleague. The fact I couldn't find the man's wallet, which he must have had if he paid with cash and used a credit card, furthered my curiosity.

'I need your help to lift the body.'

'Shouldn't we wait until the crime scene boys get here?'

'No,' I said, 'I have a feeling there's something under him, a message of some kind.'

My colleague gave me a quizzical look but agreed to help. We rolled the body on its side and there under it was an envelope.

'How the fuck did you know that?' said my colleague, clearly spooked.

I reached for the envelope and seeing the top lip had been folded carefully into the envelope's pocket, I pried it open gently. Inside there was a single sheet of paper and a brief handwritten note which read:

This is the only good way to end this. We can both rest now.

My colleague leaned in and read the words slowly, his lips moving as he read. We stood there in silence. I tried to piece together a narrative which would explain the events, but couldn't get past the fact the door had been blocked with a door stopper from the inside. I began to feel a sense of unease as if someone were looking at me and turned to look over my right shoulder. The black-haired girl in the plum-coloured school uniform stood there. She was smiling at me. She lifted her hand and waved at me before turning and running out the door. I immediately followed her, but when I got to the door, she was gone.

'What's wrong with you?' said my colleague.

I stepped into the corridor and looked up and down. The security men kept their eyes straight ahead. I was about to ask them if they'd seen the girl, but I knew what they'd say. I re-entered into the room and told my colleague to bag the note as I was going home to spend time with my wife and grandson. Before I left, I turned to him and told him the crime scene unit would find no prints other than the dead man's. I don't know why I said it, it just came out. In the days after the discovery, I didn't spend much time thinking about the impossibility of his death. There was nothing else to do except write it up and follow what leads we could, though I doubted they'd go anywhere.

A month after the body's discovery, we hit a dead end and I decided to retire. I'd had enough and knew the case would go on and on and sap whatever energy remained in my body. Bill Price took over the case and I retreated into a quiet, uneventful life. Bill and I went a long way back, and he told me occasional details about how the investigation was progressing from time to time. One Sunday, about four months after I'd quit, we met for a pint in The Gravediggers beside Glasnevin Cemetery. I know I said I didn't have the energy for a case like this one, but what had prompted me to abandon it were the repeated visits from the dark-haired girl. I'd see her almost every day, usually when I was trying to think things through. I be sitting alone, looking unobtrusively out the window when she'd appear in my peripheral vision and then, she'd stand before me, unmoving, just looking at me. I tried ignoring her, but she kept coming back, so I asked her what she wanted but received no answer. A few days afterward, I told her I couldn't help her, and I was l retiring. Her face changed when I related this to her. She took a step towards me and for a moment, I thought she was going to do something to me, but she stopped and disappeared.

I never saw her again after that.

Bill and I drank the first pint slowly and chatted about our families, the weather, and the football. It wasn't until we were on the third pint, Bill relaxed enough to tell me what he'd discovered. Before I'd decided to quit, we'd established the dead man had used a false name and stolen credit card when checking into the hotel. The autopsy revealed he'd died of suffocation, and there were no drugs or alcohol in his system. A forensic analysis of the room found nothing. There were no fibres of note, and every fingerprint could be attributed to the dead man or to hotel staff. Though none of us investigating the case said it out loud, we were all bewildered and even upset by its impossibility. By that time, the story was national news and its presence permeated everything in the department from the bottom to the top. I could see it in the drawn faces of my colleagues and how their eyes all had the same far-away look.

David Scott's body remained in the morgue until a week before Bill and I met in The Gravediggers. No one had come forward to claim the body, despite a nationwide campaign to identify him. Then one morning, things changed. A package arrived at the Chief Pathologist's office. It mentioned the dead man, though it didn't give his name and included details of his death, including the room number and what he was wearing. Inside the package, which had been wrapped carefully and delivered by registered post, was a box. Inside the box was enough cash to cover a funeral and a card which simply read:

*Yours ever, Erica*

'I don't get it,' said Bill.

'I don't think there's anything to get,' I said, 'some questions aren't meant to be answered.'

Bill took out a notebook and a plastic bag, inside which there was a card of some kind.

'That's very philosophical, but it's not much use to me.'

We shared a laugh. Then Bill put on his reading glasses and scanned his notes.

'When was he buried?'

'On Thursday,' said Bill.

'We're you there?'

'A few of us went, hoping she'd turn up.'

'Is that the card?' I asked, motioning towards the plastic bag.

Bill slid it across the table to me.

'Prints?'

Bill shook his head.

The handwriting was the same as the note in the hotel.

Bill and I had another pint before parting. We didn't speak about the case again, and a few months later it was officially considered cold and has remained so in the ten years since.

Two days ago, after I'd come home from visiting my wife, I received a call on my landline. I was surprised to hear the phone ringing as almost everyone I know uses mobile phones and the only person who used the landline was my wife, but she hadn't lived in the house for almost a year. I'd never bothered getting the phone disconnected. It was all part of whatever deal my son set up with the internet company. All I know about those things is I pay a bill every month and I can watch sports on TV and browse the web when I'm inclined to, which isn't often. I picked up the phone. At first, there was silence, and then I heard a voice, *a child's voice, a girl's voice,* as if it were all around me, swirling in the air of the hallway. Abruptly, the voice fractured and began echoing, as if a gust of wind was carrying it away. I strained to listen, but couldn't make out what was being said. And then, the line became silent. I stood there for a long time trying to recall what I'd heard, or even if I'd heard anything. After plumbing the depths of my mind until there was nowhere left to go, I gave up trying to recover the message and went to bed. As I lay in the dark, I began to long for a visitation from Erica, for her to deliver her message in person, but she didn't come.

I must have passed out at some point during the night, and when I woke, a faint and honeyed sliver of light bisected the room. I lay there and started to work my way through the alphabet, thinking of words beginning with each letter. It was an old trick I'd learned from a colleague years before. The act was a kind of meditation, focusing the mind and supposedly allowed buried information to rise to the surface by dredging my subconscious depths. I must have been there for twenty minutes before a name began to form. During my walk through the alphabet, I kept stumbling on the letter L which after some thought became the name Lorcan and then the letter N which became the name, Nolan. I couldn't place the name within any investigation or conversation I'd had, but something told me I'd heard the name on the phone from the night before. I got up, showered, and dressed and took the dog for a walk. I then drove to my former place of employment and was grateful to see Wally Keegan on the desk. Wally wouldn't ask questions. I asked him if I could check something in the records. He made a quip about me being retired before giving me access to the basement. I descended the dark steps and felt the cold air creep into my bones. I knew exactly what I was looking for and within the hour I had found it.

Lorcan Nolan was abandoned at birth, presumably because he'd been born out of wedlock, and left with the nuns where he stayed as an infant until finally ending up in the boys' reformatory my daughter had mentioned when Erica had first appeared to her almost forty years before. Nolan must have grown up and been employed somewhere, but I couldn't find any employment record or even a PPS number. It was as if this man never existed beyond childhood, and yet, I'd seen his dead body there in a quiet, interior room in the Gresham. I thought about the tragedy of his life, his abandonment at birth and the cruel fact of his lonely and terrifying death. I also thought about Erica and whose bones had been unearthed all those years before. I had ideas, but as I said before, none of them made any rational sense, but then again, why did things have to make rational sense? I remember reading how science is the best toolkit we have for explaining the world, but how it is also incomplete and even though that creates maddening uncertainty, I have to live with that fact in much the same way the doctors who treat my wife cannot explain the mechanism which causes the proteins in her brain to misfold and build up, killing the neurons which make her mind work.

Earlier today I visited her. We had a nice time; I brought the dog, and we strolled around the grounds. Walking is very pleasant this time of year, and today was particularly good. The chalky sky from earlier in the morning had brightened into a pale Uranian blue, and the sun sat as a watery splash of yellow high in the midday coolness. We sat on a clean and comfortable bench. I told my wife about our children and grandchildren and the day-to-day mundanity of our lives. She smiled, but I knew behind her eyes was a gulf which swallowed up my words and mangled them into unintelligible noise. She held the dog's face and rubbed his ears while his tail wagged like a furious metronome. I took her hand and there it sat passively, almost weightless, in mine while I squeezed it gently. We sat there contentedly until a nurse came to take my wife to lunch. I thanked her, kissed my wife goodbye, and made my way along the gravel path to my car. I was about ten yards or so from my car when one of my wife's doctors, a tall young woman with big green eyes and a warm smile which was genuine rather than the affectation so many of her colleagues adopted, approached me.

'I'm sorry,' she said, 'I had hoped to talk to you, but I didn't want to interrupt your time with your wife.'

The dog jumped up on her in his playful, affectionate way, and she rubbed him on the head.

'He likes people,' I said, apologetically.

'Dogs are very intuitive.'

I smiled and nodded. I waited for her to say what she wanted to say. In the silence, I feared the worst. Though there were no signs of improvement in my wife, I hadn't seen any further decline either. Perhaps they had found something else, a tumour or heart murmur, something which would hasten her departure from this world. I felt the cold electricity of fear ripple through my chest.

'Is there someone in your family named Erica?'

I don't know how I must have appeared to her, but her face showed concern.

'No,' I said, finally, my voice scratchy as if the word scraped the inside of my throat.

'Your wife has mentioned the name several times in the last couple of days. I thought it might be the name of a relative or friend. Has she said anything to you?'

'No, but my daughter had an imaginary friend named Erica when she was a child.'

The doctor smiled with perfunctory politeness. It told me she had her answer and there would be no more questions.

'Goodbye, doctor,' I said, 'thank you for taking care of my wife.'

We exchanged a kindly smile.

From out of nowhere, a small but powerful wind kicked up, scattering the early autumn leaves. The dog began to chase the yellow and red leaves as they spun in tiny eddies in the October air. Somewhere in the distance, I thought I saw movement between the trees. I'm not sure what it was, and I've tried not to think about, but somehow, I know it will be part of me for whatever years I have left, and maybe even longer than that.

# THE ENORMOUS CAT

Helen Latimer's husband, George, died just before lunch on an overcast Tuesday in June. He had been in the garden tending his roses when he felt a sudden tightness in his chest followed by a wave of light-headedness followed by oblivion. His final earthly sensation, other than the wrenching squeeze which took his breath away, was the light and powdery sweetness of his roses.

For forty years they were his pride and joy, and it seemed fitting that fate decree he die among them. As he was leaving the corporeal world, Helen called him from the kitchen to ask what type of sandwich he wanted. She thought nothing of it when he didn't reply. George was taciturn to a fault, and doubly so when gardening. After a brief time, Helen, growing impatient, decided to venture out and repeat the question to his face. It was rare, but not unheard of, that he ignored a question to his face. George could pretend not to hear things as well as any man. As she made her way to the garden, Helen caught sight of her face reflected in French doors. She thought she looked tired, even for a woman of her age. A half-formed thought about living with George all these years flashed through her mind, but she paid it no heed and when it vanished, she was unsure there had been a thought to begin with.

'George, are you there?' she called as she walked towards the high shrubs which formed a green wall around the sun trap of their patio.

She expected he was pottering around in his shed among the copious jars and boxes, looking for this or that. He spent more time there than anywhere else. In the forty-two years they'd been married, not a day had passed, when George had not, on some pretext or another, managed to sequester himself in his shed with his radio.

At first, it hadn't bothered Helen. She was young and, in those days, it was best if a wife didn't bother her husband when he wanted to be alone. She'd gone into the marriage with open eyes. George's mother had warned her all about his funny ways. These funny ways were attractive quirks at first, but it didn't take all that long for them to become the reason she would sometimes find herself looking out the window, biting her nails, and thinking thoughts unbecoming of a wife. In the middle and later years of their life together, Helen learned to ignore her frustration and took to drinking wine and going on long walks. Now in the twilight of their marriage, she simply didn't care. George was what he was. And that was that.

It was with such thoughts swirling in her mind like odd socks in a dryer, she set eyes on her dead husband. She knew he was dead straight away. He lay sprawled across his Pink Knockouts and Carefree Spirits with the most peculiar look on his face. It was as if someone had given him a great fright or told him a wonderful joke. He was gripping his secateurs so tightly it looked like they would snap. Helen sighed, returned inside and called for an ambulance.

After the ambulance arrived and took George away, Mrs. Byrne from next door dropped in. A small group had gathered on the street, and Mrs. Byrne had appointed herself to act on its behalf. Helen received her without enthusiasm.

'A cup of tea,' said Mrs. Byrne, 'that's what you need.'

Helen smiled benignly as Mrs. Byrne busied herself by rifling through presses for cups and tea bags and other such things. Helen couldn't remember when Mrs. Byrne, or any neighbours for that matter, had last been for a cup of tea. George didn't like the neighbours. He found them intrusive and nosey, and they found him surly and unfriendly. It didn't matter anymore. George was dead and Helen, bereft of his protection, would have to sit like a crumpled piece of paper and endure the kindness of Mrs. Byrne.

'The Lord only calls us when we are ready,' said Mrs. Byrne.

Helen smiled politely, but didn't care for such potted stoicism. It was clear to her The Lord in his wisdom didn't appreciate lunch. George might have enjoyed a sandwich before leaving for the great hereafter.

Mrs. Byrne rabbited on about how hard it would be without George, especially as Helen and George had no children. She then suggested, in the same breathless drivel, Helen call Fr. Hourihane and book the church for the funeral. Helen's eyes began to wander beyond her neighbour's face and into the garden's verdant abundance, which she noted was all hers now. While lost in these thoughts, she noticed something moving along the back wall. A tiny shape emerged from the variegated colours and fell with the delicacy of a ballerina onto the manicured grass. Mrs. Byrne, oblivious to Helen's enchantment with this mysterious object, yapped on almost without drawing breath and barely noticed when Helen arose and moved to the window.

'What is it?' asked Mrs. Byrne after a moment.

Helen said nothing. She stepped through the French doors and into the garden.

Mrs. Byrne moved slowly towards the window. She peeked into the garden, where she saw Helen kneeling on the grass. Thinking Helen was praying, she attributed this connection with The Lord to her own wise counsel. She finished her tea with a slurp and, feeling a sense of accomplishment, decided her works of spiritual mercy were complete and that Helen's wellbeing was now the responsibility of others.

Outside, Helen stared into the bluest eyes she'd ever seen. They looked like little cloudless skies. After a moment, she spoke to their owner.

'Where have you come from?' she whispered.

The cat, which was grey and white and no bigger than a closed fist, blinked twice and yawned, revealing two rows of perfect, tiny white teeth.

'You must be hungry,' said Helen.

She stood up and went back to the house and was surprised to find the cat following at her heels. A pang of anxiety struck her. The cat was so small, she worried she'd step on it, but when she opened the door, and it hopped into the house with the alacrity of a schoolchild on the first day of summer, all nervousness left her. Her instincts were to give the cat milk, but she recalled reading somewhere how milk could upset a cat's stomach, and given this cat was so small, she thought it better to give it something else. Thinking hard as to what she could feed it, she remembered George had enjoyed a tuna sandwich every now and then, and seeing as he was no longer around, the tuna may as well go to another mouth. She retrieved a can from the pantry, opened it, and spooned out about a third of its contents onto a plate. She watched with fascination as the cat consumed the tuna in a single, impossible, mouthful.

'You must be really famished,' said Helen, bending down to spoon out the remaining tuna.

The cat gobbled it up in about ten seconds, then licked its lips, first one way and then the other. It then rubbed its head with its paw and, once done grooming itself, hopped onto a kitchen chair with the casual nonchalance of a familiar guest. Once there, it curled into the shape of a Danish pastry and fell asleep.

Helen smiled in a mix of bemusement and the unfamiliar feeling of joy. Something about the cat reminded her of George, but she put it down to the fact everything reminded her of George, the house, the garden, the roses, the shed — especially the shed. She began to wonder where the cat had come from. It appeared too small to have lost its mother, and so she surmised its mother was around somewhere, or perhaps its mother was dead or injured and the little thing had ventured into the world following its instinct to survive. Whatever it was, the cat was asleep in her house and Helen was happy to have this little visitor to share her home with. She left the cat to sleep and walked into the hall to call Fr. Hourihane.

The conversation lasted an hour, though Helen felt it had lasted at least twice that. Fr. Hourihane liked to talk and waxed lyrical about George's love of his garden, travel, and sport. Helen felt like objecting when Fr. Hourihane spoke of travel. Travel was *her* love. Had George gotten his way, they would never have left Dublin. It occurred to Helen, and not for the first time, as Fr. Hourihane rattled on and on, about how uneventful her life had been and how she'd sacrificed so much for George and got so little in return. If only they'd been blessed with children, she thought for the millionth time, glancing to the blank wall where photographs of grandchildren might have hung. But fate dealt them a cruel hand. George could make anything grow in a garden, but a childhood bout of mumps had left him as sterile as an Arctic landscape. Still, life is what you make it, and Helen found some comfort in her few friends, her city breaks (usually without George) and her love of art and art galleries. Every week, sometimes more than once, she took herself into the city to visit an art galleries or museum. George never showed an interest in such things and would scoff at the notion of appreciating stuff which was, as he put it, made up.

'I mean,' he would say proudly as he made a delicate cut along the plum-red stem of a pink rose, 'this is art, the stuff you gawk at can't hold a candle to this. Nature is the real artist.' Helen acknowledged he had a point, but George became smug and affected an air of superiority which said he knew best. Helen raised her eyes to heaven and left him to it. She didn't care for people who were smug.

One afternoon, Helen came home to find George asleep in his armchair. This was part of his routine, and she smiled in appreciation of his ways. Sometimes they were endearing. However, such sentiments left her as soon as she noticed he'd been careless and had dragged mud into the house. Instead of waking him and admonishing him, which was pointless, she went into the garden and snapped three of his Teasing Georgias.

'I know it seems hard to understand now,' droned Fr. Hourihane, wrenching Helen back to reality, 'but the Lord has his reasons.'

'Thank you, Father, I have to go.'

She hung up, deciding she needed a glass of water.

When she entered the kitchen, the cat was still asleep, but
something strange had happened. Instead of it lying there curled
up like a tiny comma, it was now the size of a full-grown cat.
Helen scrunched her face and squinted hard as if to correct any
defect in her vision, but the cat was cat-sized and purring softly
like an idling engine. A moment later, it opened its eyes and gave
a ferocious yawn followed by a resonant and trilling miaow. The
cat pounced from the chair and curled itself around Helen's legs
like smoke. Helen stood motionless, but her eyes took in the
creature's length. Its lithe body was powerful, and its tail moved
like a dancer. She bent down to stroke it, and it bumped its head
against her hand and rubbed its cheeks along her wrist. The softness of its fur felt soothing on her skin.

'I must be losing my mind as well as my eyesight,' said Helen
quietly.

Over the next few days, the cat ate and slept and grew steadily
bigger. By the end of the week, it was the size of a golden re-
triever. After the initial shock, Helen delighted in seeing the cat
every morning and observing how much bigger it had gotten.

'Look at you,' she would say, 'you're almost too big for the
chair.'

The following day, the cat had moved from the chair to the
couch.

Within a week, the cat was the size of a lion, and Helen began
to grow concerned about what to do with it. She didn't feel
threatened or worried for her safety, indeed even with its great
and unusual size, the cat was as gentle and affectionate as when
she'd first encountered it. No, her concern was her neighbours,
and after that, the rest of the world. She thought about calling the
zoo but began to worry they would take the cat away and study
it. Whoever she thought to call, she knew it had the possibility of

ending badly for the cat. She decided to do nothing, accepting instead the strangeness of the situation and how it was best left unencumbered by any practical issues.

The cat must have sensed Helen's concern, as it began to spend less time in the house. It would lie among George's roses and sleep during the day, or sometimes take itself to the empty shed. In the week after George's death, his nephews had come over and taken away anything of use or value they could find. Helen didn't mind, they were welcome to it. They paid her no notice, were briskly polite, and soon on their way with a car full of junk. They were all the same, those Latimers, it was a pity she had devoted her life to one of them. Anyway, now they had what they wanted and were gone, she was glad to see the back of them. It was the end of her relationship with them. At the funeral, George's brother and his wife barely spoke with Helen and had no dealings with her since, apart from mention of a pending solicitor's letter to view George's will.

One morning, about a month after the cat's arrival, the roses George had cultivated with such care and love lay flattened on the ground. Helen couldn't help but smile when she noticed. She walked to the shed to feed the cat, only to find it was now too big to get out the door.

'Oh dear,' she said, 'what shall I do with you?'

She knew it was time to call an expert.

Like mould on bread, a media circus grew up around her home. At first, it was a chap from the RSPCA, but within an hour of him seeing the cat, there were four others, and a day later the TV people descended like low pressure from the Atlantic.

By this time, the cat almost filled the shed's interior, and despite the clamour which had grown up around it, the cat slept and purred contentedly, appearing unaffected by everything. Occasionally, it would stir and stretch, and the shed would shake and look as if it would rise from the ground, only to settle once more to the delight and relief of those gathered. Only the neighbourhood boys revelled in pure excitement and would whoop and dare each other to go to the shed door and touch the cat. Helen enjoyed their good-natured and innocent curiosity. The media, however, was another thing. They were a nuisance. They rang Helen's doorbell and thrust microphones and cameras in her face. They asked her inane questions, and for the first time since George's death, she missed him. He would have known how to deal with them.

One evening in July, the doorbell rang, and Helen answered it expecting to find someone from RTE or Sky News, but instead she found Fr. Hourihane. He wasted no time in letting himself into the house, and within a few minutes was talking about signs and wonders and The Lord and mysteries and all sorts of other hocus-pocus. Helen paid no attention to his notions and smiled politely as he gesticulated and quoted scripture. She admitted to herself a curiosity regarding the cat's provenance and why it grew to such a size, but she had never considered anything supernatural about it, not because she didn't believe in such things but because the whole thing was, on some level, perfectly normal.

Fr. Hourihane, filled with a sense of fiery righteousness, made his way to the shed and approached the door. The neighbourhood boys sat on the wall between the houses and held their breath as the priest poked his head around the door. He stood in amazement and was marvelling at the creature when, without warning, the cat yawned. A terrified Fr. Hourihane fell backwards and clawed a retreat with the haste of someone in mortal peril. He managed to roll over and, once on his feet, ran with Olympic speed into the house and out the front door. The boys on the wall laughed aloud like a chorus of jackdaws. Helen, drawn to the noise, went out to the boys.

'Your cat is brilliant, Mrs. Latimer,' said a blond-haired boy.

'I bet Fr. Hourihane has to change his underpants,' said another.

The boys guffawed and Helen smiled in appreciation of their humour, even if it was a bit crude for her tastes. She returned to the house and soon after reappeared with biscuits and cake. The boys slid down from the wall like thick syrup and graciously accepted the food.

'Are they going to take the cat away?' asked a boy.

'I don't know,' said Helen, 'I don't even know if they can. The people from the zoo are talking with some people about it.'

'I hope they don't take it away,' said a boy, 'it's the best thing around here.'

Helen forced a smile. She knew there were plans to remove the cat the next morning. She regretted lying to the boys, but she didn't want to spoil their enjoyment.

At that moment, the cat let out a loud miaow which shook the shed and reverberated along the walls of the neighbouring houses.

'Maybe he's hungry,' said the blond-haired boy.

Helen left the boys to their munching and searched through her cupboards for food for the cat. In the chaos surrounding the miracle moggie, she had not fed it as regularly as before. Oddly, this did not affect the cat nor its size in any way. The cat was now so big, all food it received were mere morsels. She came back into the garden as the lengthy shadows of dusk began to move along it. In the shed, the cat purred contentedly. Helen carried the open can of tuna to the door and emptied it onto a plate. It was the last tin in the pantry. Helen thought it fitting given the cat would soon be gone. The cat's nose twitched, and its eyes opened. It moved its huge head to the door and pushed its muzzle into the air. Helen gestured for the boys to gather around. They did so with a patient and orderly obedience, and then they began rubbing the cat's nose and stroking its whiskers.

'Mrs. Latimer,' said one of the boys, his fingers running through the cat's soft fur, 'do you think the cat is magic?'

'I don't know,' said Helen, 'what do you think?'

'I told my cousin about it, but he didn't believe me.'

'Didn't he see it on the news?' asked Helen.

'He said it was fake.'

Helen placed the plate of tuna before the cat's huge mouth, and it lapped it up in one lick and then closed its eyes. It purred, and the rhythmic reverberations enveloped Helen and the boys in a wonderful sense of calm. They stayed with it until the edges of the evening emerged, and it began to grow dark.

Despite this calm, Helen did not sleep well. She wrestled with a fitful sleep, and just as she nodded off, somewhere in the liminal space between sleep and dreams, she heard a tremendous crash, which startled her awake. She got up and hurried to the back room as the noise had come from the garden. She could see a large rectangular shape moving clumsily in the dark. It was the shed. It had risen from the ground and now had four huge limbs, a long and powerful tail, and a thick square head thrust through the splintering wood. In an instant, the shed had disintegrated, and the cat, now the size of an elephant, sat in Helen Latimer's back garden, licking its paw as if time had stood still. It looked up towards her and through the night's starry grey, Helen once again saw the blue sparkle of the cat's eyes. It blinked slowly, and with a graceful bound, leaped over the wall and was gone.

No one knew where the cat went or heard anything about it ever again, and soon all interest in Helen Latimer and the cat disappeared and moved onto something else. In time, people would claim there never was an enormous cat, while others would say the cat's size was over-exaggerated. Some said it was an escaped lion from the zoo, and others said it was a dog.

A few days after the cat's departure, there was a knock at Helen's door. It was the group of boys. They stood before her, silent and respectful. None of them spoke, but none of them needed to say anything.

Helen smiled.

'I think I have some more biscuits somewhere in the pantry,' she said, inviting them inside.

# THE FAWN

It was the fifth city in five years, and it was his turn to choose. He scanned a map of Europe and landed lazily on what was convenient rather than meaningful. Had he given it more thought he'd have found a narrative to thread through his choice, but this year was different? He tried, but couldn't place the exact centre of difference. *Was it the tone of her voice when they'd spoken on the phone the week before that was different.* He thought she sounded distant, like someone lost in a daydream.

He'd long ago stopped trying to interpret words between lovers like a teenager's heart's agitations, and ignored her aloof tone. He occasionally overthought things, imagining spectres lurking in shadows he'd created within his mind, but this time there was something there, like a word snatched from a half-heard conversation, faint and unclear, but there. He feared the worst but pretended he didn't.

Distraction was present in his body and mind, taking the intangible form of a nagging discomfort. A dull ache caught him off guard and forced him to take a deep breath and drive deep into his past where the scars of youthful romances lingered. It sent tight quivers through his chest and subdued the yearning he felt for her. He was tired but couldn't relax while the plane trundled along, building up momentum before the final thrust of take-off.

'Barcelona,' his wife had said to him earlier that day, 'these conferences take you to such lovely places. Where were you last year again?'

'Berlin,' he said, trying to conceal the furtive tone he was sure spilled from his lips like blood from a wound.

She smiled softly, as if berating herself for not remembering.

'Of course, Berlin, my memory is so bad. How could I forget when you came back so refreshed and energised?'

'It was a nice trip,' he said.

'Have you got everything, tickets, passport, socks, underwear?'

He nodded in the way he'd practised, giving her the right amount of naturalism. Every time he told her he was going away to attend a conference, the lie caught in his throat like a fishbone. Later, when alone, he could rationalise it by telling himself it was only once a year and what she didn't know wouldn't harm her and, besides, who wasn't entitled to a little bit of secrecy in their lives.

'Are you sure you don't want a lift?'

'No, thanks, I'll hop on the bus," he said, leaning in to kiss her perfunctorily on the cheek before adding, 'I'll bring you back something nice.'

She smiled, there was still light in her eyes, like vestiges of day on an autumn evening. He'd always brought her back something nice. Not flashy or expensive, but thoughtful. One year it was a watch, another a pair of earbuds, and another a perfume she liked.

The plane rose into the air, wobbling as it buffeted the currents swirling around it. He looked out the window at the shrinking world below. Selena's face flashed across his mind, followed by his wife's face before finally settling on Selena's once more. Any feelings of guilt had evaporated long ago. The first morning he'd awoken beside Selena and wondered what he was doing, he'd noticed he'd given himself permission to be there. Over the next few days, he'd wrestled with the idea, finally conquering his scruples, and running headlong into whatever was to come.

With the plane taking a steep bank to the left, he began to re-call the first time he'd met Selena. It was a coffee break from the day's business, and he was standing around, keeping his distance from the others. He hated these things, a lot of people saying nothing about nothing important and thinking they were impor-tant while doing it. He hated shoptalk. The publishing business was full of people with avid attitudes about new horizons and how the digital space was opening new markets. He was old school, and the future of print worried him deeply. Lost in thought, the surface of reality suddenly loomed up at him, jarred into the present by a voice coming from inside his head. The voice was sibilant and rolled with music.

'Sorry, but your tie is askew.'

The first thing he noticed was her eyes. They were deep and brown and shone with the auburn tint of chestnuts. She looked at him the way he wanted to be looked at, as if she knew him exact-ly. Every secret of his heart exposed without judgement of his faults. A pretty smile spread across her face, like time expanding into a warm afternoon. Her hair was shoulder-length, but the cut was distinct, not something he'd seen before. She was in her late thirties, perhaps early forties, it was hard to tell. She was both classic and timeless. Her skin was youthful, and energy radiated from her, but something about her eyes tripped the switches of his mind and stumbled his thought.

'Do you mind?' she asked.

Before he could answer, she had leaned into him and straight-ened his tie with deft and delicate hands. She held on to his tie just a moment longer than acceptable and looked into his eyes and waited. He wanted to kiss her.

'Normally, my wife would do it for me.'

'That's the trouble with men of a certain age,' she said with matronly coolness, 'you become like little boys without your wives or mothers to look after you.'

'What age do you think I am?' he asked.

She regarded him matter-of-factly, took in his posture, greying hair and, tie aside, smart, tailored suit.

'I'd say early fifties, but I don't know. You look like you've aged well.'

'Early fifties work for me.'

'I'm Selena,' she said, offering her hand.

'Goddess of the moon,' he said quietly, before quickly and awkwardly saying, 'Tom.'

She regarded the name tag, which hung at right angles on his lapel.

'Tom Newland,' she read while straightening the tag, 'where are you from, Tom Newland?'

'Dublin.'

Her head tilted ever so slightly to the left and a wrinkle crossed her forehead as if she were trying to solve a complicated arithmetic problem.

'Did I say something wrong?'

'No. I used to know a guy from Dublin.'

'That bad, huh?'

'You could say that' she replied, 'it's a long story.'

'We have time.'

A moment of silence fell between them like a hummingbird visiting a feeder. After taking a drink, it flitted off and words returned to fill the space.

'I'm not an expert on accents, but I'd guess you were from Boston,' he said, his voice rising into a question laden with uncertainty as if he were reaching into something whose bottom he couldn't see.

'You're good,' she said, her smile was wide, and her eyes twinkled, 'A little north of Boston. I'm from Danvers, Massachusetts.'

'Why does that name ring a bell?'

Her eyes probed his eyes as if she were trying to communicate telepathically with him. An idea began to form in his mind, emerging into clarity like a distant figure coming into view.

'Salem,' he said finally, 'isn't Danvers near Salem, where the witch trials took place?'

'Full marks for both history and geography,' she said playfully, 'have you ever been?'

'No, I did amateur dramatics when I was in college, we did a production of *The Crucible*. It was a long time ago.'

'Wow, that explains why you're such a practised speaker. You must have been a good actor.'

'I can't tell if you're being sarcastic or not.'

'Oh, you'd know if I was being sarcastic, you'd really know,' she said, fixing him a stare and then smiling warmly, 'what part did you play?'

'Hale.'

'I'd have guessed Proctor.'

'I wasn't that good.'

'You're actually about the same age as the historical Proctor, Miller's character was about twenty years younger.'

'You seem to know a lot, were you there?'

She laughed, then flicked out her fingers at his face and mumbled something. Emboldened by her sense of fun, he asked her if she was a witch.

'I was, my membership got revoked last year,' she said before adding with perfect drollness, 'it was a real bummer because I had to take a plane to get here.'

He was hooked. They laughed at the joke and in that instant, he felt he'd known her all his life. This small talk felt so different to the chatter he engaged in with colleagues and friends and his wife. This felt much bigger somehow, as if he had been connected to a world of infinite possibilities. He could have stayed there forever, but his reverie was broken by the coordinator's booming voice calling everyone back into the conference room.

'Better get back to it.'

'I know,' sighed Selena, 'have you been to a more boring conference?'

'Probably, but I can't remember.'

'They all seem to roll into an endless monotony like …'

'Rain in October,' he said, finishing her sentence.

Her eyes told him he'd anticipated her comparison word for word.

Just then, without warning, she moved away with the fluidity of one movie scene blending into the next. He watched her go and wondered what had happened.

After the seminar, rather than retreating to the sanctuary of his room, he risked the bar's raucous chaos, hoping to see Selena. The strange mix of awkwardness and ease he'd felt during their brief encounter had occupied his mind the whole afternoon. He couldn't recall anything about trends in modern publication, despite giving the second part of his presentation on the Irish market. He knew he'd fielded questions and answered them. It was as if there were a veil over his memory. He ordered a whisky and after drinking half of it in one gulp, he moved around the bright room and experienced the unquiet gauche of a teenager at their first house party. More than once he bumped into people who he'd met on the first morning. They knew his name, but he couldn't bring theirs to mind. He smiled politely when they complimented his presentation but realising his search for Selena was futile, he excused himself, saying he was tired and had to call his wife.

Lying on the bed back in his room a short time after leaving the bar, Tom took out his phone and searched for the group email containing the day's itinerary sent the night before. He read down through the list of names and, after a moment, found Selena's email address. Selenaabigailpickman@mercypublishing.de. *Germany*, he thought. She hadn't told him where she was based in Europe. He Googled Mercy Publishing and discovered it was mostly an academic publisher of history textbooks. He found Selena's bio and noted she had an MA in history from the University of Amherst, and she'd been with the company for almost ten years. He wrote a brief message asking her if she wanted to meet for a drink. His thumb hovered over the send button, and before he could talk himself out of sending the invitation, he pressed send and felt the sudden rush of panic and excitement which compelled him to recoil as if from an electric shock.

It didn't take long for Selena to reply. She told him she was out to dinner with colleagues, but would be back at the hotel later that evening. She added the proviso that she was tired and wouldn't be good company, but she'd be happy to meet him the following evening. He lay back on the mounds of pillows the hotel thought their guests needed for some reason and sank into the frustration of delayed gratification. Telling himself to grow up, he laughed and flicked on the television and watched the news. He tried to pay attention to whatever breaking story was featured but became restless. He decided to call his wife.

'Hi,' he said.

'Hi,' replied his wife, 'are you enjoying yourself?'

They exchanged the simple and familiar words of small talk, and a sense of calm returned to him, soothing the waters of his recently upturned world.

'Any word from Julia?' he asked.

'Yes, she sent me a text about an hour ago telling me she'd landed.'

'Don't worry about her, do you hear me?'

'I'll try not to.'

He pulled his phone away from his face and took a deep breath before returning to the conversation.

'I'm sure she'll have a great time, now promise me you won't worry, she'll be fine, and she's with her friends.'

'I hope you're right, it's a little strange having the house to myself.'

'You have Paddock.'

Paddock, a mercurial seven-year-old black cat, moved through their lives like a shadow. A presence more than substance, he flitted in and out of the house in the perpetual nomadic lifestyle of a creature which lived between spaces.

'He's at the kitchen window, I think I'll let him in and then make myself some tea.'

While more small talk filled their conversation, he heard the soft beep of a newly delivered email and his heart skipped. He forced himself to wait patiently while his wife spoke and then once it was his turn to speak, he steered the conversation towards its conclusion. A few minutes later, he read Selena's email. It was direct. It was her room number. An hour later, they were in bed.

It had begun.

\*

London, Paris, Venice, Berlin and now Barcelona. Five years before, when the ritual had begun, he'd taken a chance, and it had worked. On the final day, they travelled to the airport together. Selena told him she lived in Würzburg, and had been in a relationship until relatively recently, and was now happily single and living her best life. Over a coffee, while they waited to go their respective ways, they agreed to stay in touch.

'Just casual,' he said, 'no pressure.'

'Until next time,' she said.

By the time he'd got back to Dublin, he'd already devised a pretext to meet her. There were the usual exchanges on WhatsApp and the occasional email. It was banter, meaningless back-and-forth, nothing to suggest there was a burgeoning romance. While this was going on, his thoughts were becoming increasingly scattered. It was as if Selena had conjured a storm, and he was at its epicentre. He found it difficult to concentrate at work, and was even more remote at home. His wife, who looked to avoid any confrontation, ignored the development, explaining it away as work-related stress. He was forever complaining about work and how busy he was and how much pressure there was to keep up with emerging trends.

'Why don't you do something else?' she said, 'you're still young.'

'I'm fifty-five,' he said in resignation, 'I've been doing this since I was twenty-three. I wouldn't know what to do.'

'Why don't you get back to writing your book?' she said, and regretted it immediately.

He looked at her with the searing contempt of someone who'd been betrayed.

'I'm sorry,' she said.

He left the room and apart from day-to-day domestic matters, they didn't speak for almost a week.

The book she'd referred to was one of the many albatrosses he'd attached to the narrative of his failure. He'd tried and tried to get it off the ground, but each time he'd thought he was nearing escape velocity, the engines stuttered and whatever momentum he'd gained petered out and the project flopped once more to the hard ground of unrealised dreams.

*It's a great idea, Tom, it's just not what we're looking for.*

*I know what we're looking for, I work for this company.*

*I know that, Tom, but believe me, this isn't going to work, sometimes even the best ideas are not worth the risk.*

He'd hawked his proposal and several opening chapters to friends in the industry, but all he found was polite interest, platitudes, and proof that his ambition to publish a book through traditional means was not going to happen.

*Why don't you try publishing it yourself? Amazon has a great platform for that kind of thing.*

About six months after they'd first met, he sent Selena an email with a plane ticket to London attached and the name of a hotel.

*I'll be there from the 21st-26th. My wife thinks I'm going to a conference. It'd be great if you could make it.*

She replied within the hour.

*I'll be there.*

As he waited in the lounge for her to arrive, a cacophony of doubts arose in his mind. An unsettling feeling rippled through him like a cold wind. He couldn't comprehend exactly what was happening and each time he tried to articulate his thoughts within his conscious narrative they collapsed into a muddle of fragments like leaves swirling in autumnal eddies. And then she was there, sliding into the seat across from him, her eyes twinkling and her lips full and red and slightly parted.

\*

Just under a year later, Selena chose Paris for their next tryst. They spent five days in hedonistic delight. On the final day, they visited Père Lachaise. Something about the place animated Selena in a way he'd not seen before. She would touch the grey stone of graves and mausoleums in what he could only describe as an intimate fashion. It was as if she were drawing power from them.

'Give me your hand,' she said as she leaned on the side of Théodore Géricault's tomb. Her face was pressed into the pallid green oxide of copper relief, and her eyes were closed. Her hand searched for his. He moved over to her reluctantly, like a dog who doesn't want to come to its master. When their hands made contact, he felt a surge of energy move through him.

'You felt it, didn't you?'

He didn't respond.

'I know you did, Tom, you may as well admit it.'

'I don't know what I felt,' he said.

'Contrary to what people might think, cemeteries are full of life energy.'

'Do people think that?'

'Some.'

'I certainly don't. I think they're full of dead people.'

She opened her eyes and gave him a weary stare.

'You're no fun. I thought you'd be more open-minded.'

The following year, Tom chose Venice, ostensibly because it had no cemeteries or none which could be stumbled upon during a casual stroll. If you wanted to visit a cemetery in Venice, you had to get a boat. This didn't stop Selena from taking a solo trip to Poveglia island. She told him about the abandoned mental asylum there and how the island had been used as a quarantine station in the late 1700s.

'What's your fascination with the dead?' he asked, 'what can they possibly do for you?'

'Come with me and find out.'

He shook his head.

'Your loss,' she said, leaving the room.

\*

They met in Berlin the following year. A growing sense of importance concerning these trips had developed between them. A month after Venice, Selena had called him unexpectedly to tell him she was pregnant. The news was both exhilarating and terrifying, and for a further month until she told him she'd miscarried he existed in a mist of terror and joy. He'd met the news with immediate relief, for now, the impossible question of how to tell his wife was no longer relevant. He knew it wouldn't have ended in divorce or even separation, his wife was too traditional, too concerned with the possibility of scandal in the court of public opinion to do anything more than spend the rest of her life wondering how she'd failed so utterly as a wife. He was grateful to spare her that cruelty, cruelty, like a heat-seeking bullet, had to find a home. It flew through her, hitting him squarely in the heart.

He called Selena, suggesting a visit, but she rebuffed him. In the end, he was left to mourn in the isolation of a profound, almost primordial silence. For the rest of the year until he saw her in Berlin, he imagined the wrecked futures of a new life, another life, that which would give his current life direction. He knew he was a poor husband, and thought in a strange kind of logic that the sin of fathering a child that wasn't hers was the kind of penance he could repay in devotion to her for the rest of her life. It made sense in the dark corridors of his feelings.

It was raining heavily when he landed in Berlin. The plane skidded as it came to a stop, lurching jerkily, which caused the person sitting next to him to grab his hand so tightly their nails left a mark. He sat in the hotel lobby rubbing the scratches which had risen into an angry red welt when Selena arrived. She was wearing sunglasses despite the gloomy day and when she took them off, he saw the dark circles under her eyes. She looked older, gaunter and more etched with lines of deep sadness. When she came over to him, she didn't embrace him, instead, she reached for his hand and wrapped her fingers around his like a spider with its prey. They stayed this way for a moment before she let go of him and sat.

'You only booked one night.'

She hadn't said anything about it other than their stay in the city would be short.

'I don't like it here,' she said, 'it's a sad place.'

'Then why choose it?'

'Because it made sense given the past year,' she said with frustration and an undercurrent of resentment, 'I'll tell you tomorrow where we're going.'

He could do nothing but look at her, hoping this wasn't the time when what he knew was inevitable would happen.

'Would you prefer if I left?'

'Don't be so dramatic,' she said, the faintest trace of a nascent smile peeked out from behind her gloom, 'you're always thinking the worst.'

The next day they took the train to Würzburg. They arrived at the cusp of dusk and took a taxi to Selena's home. On the way, the Marienberg Fortress imposing silhouette loomed over them like a sentinel from a different age. He felt a powerful sense of displacement, as if he were in a tiny boat on an ocean whose size he couldn't begin to comprehend. There was something about the growing darkness which felt threatening, a feeling compounded when the taxi left the town's soft yellow streetlights and travelled into the outland's impenetrable pitch. Spidery branches of oak and alder lined the narrow road. Selena reached across and took his hand. They sat in an unsettled but stable silence. Ten minutes later, the taxi turned down a narrow road and emerged into a clearing where a cottage like something out of a fairy-tale sat fat, squat and comfortable like a plump toad.

'This is it,' said Selena.

While the house's exterior was a little odd, the inside complimented it perfectly. It was warm and homely, but also neat and ordered. There were bookcases in every room, even the downstairs bathroom, where he'd gone shortly after arriving. On top of this, there was a proliferation of plants. Streams of ivy cascaded from the top of cabinets, and each surface was bedecked with succulents and lavender. The kitchen was a garden with every herb he could think of on view. The air was warm and redolent with green and woody aromas and gave him the sense of being outside on a May afternoon instead of being inside on a chilly Autumn evening. The place was the embodiment of an optical illusion, being both cluttered and uncluttered. Selena provided no commentary to the myriad questions forming in his mind. The juxtaposition of tidiness and chaos confused him. His senses were bombarded, and he had to fight the rising claustrophobia he felt in his chest.

'I spend a lot of my life in sterile hotel rooms with their sharp artificial light and cold functionality,' said Selena, 'I've tried to create a home which is the opposite.'

*Then why did you choose me?* he thought.

They spent four days in Würzburg. After the choppy waters of Berlin, a sense of normalcy arrived on the third day. They walked along the Main and spoke like old friends and entered the space of what they were becoming. They visited the university and Selena told him about the town's history, especially its role in the persecution of women accused of witchcraft in the 1630s. They stood outside the Marienkapelle where many of those found guilty were burned at the stake.

'Burning was Europe's particular signature,' said Selena, pulling a stray strand of hair from her face as they stood in the chilly air, 'they preferred to hang them in America.'

'I have to ask.'

'It's taken you long enough,' she replied.

He waited. It was time for her to tell her truth, unvarnished and whole.

'While I was in high school, the popular girls bullied me, you know the story, death by a thousand cuts, cruelty wrapped in love. One of them, Casey Southern, was everything I was not, tall, rich, beautiful, liked by everyone, smart.'

'I can't imagine you not being beautiful or smart.'

'In school these girls squashed my confidence every day and Casey Southern was the worst. I couldn't do anything about it, and no one cared or noticed.'

'Friends, family?'

Selena laughed at his words as if she were dislodging something in her throat.

'That's for another time.'

'I have a feeling there's an end to this story.'

'Yes,' said Selena, nodding. She looked into the distance. The stray strand of hair blew across her face again, but this time she didn't reach for it.

'In my senior year, we had a new English teacher, Mrs. Montgomery. She was lovely, I really liked her, and she liked me. She sensed my distress and one day after class she asked me to stay behind. As I sat at my desk, there were sneers and comments from some of the girls. Mrs. Montgomery's face was hard like knotted wood, and she spoke with waspish sharpness when she hurried the girls from the class. I had no idea what to expect and began to feel nervous. Once the class was empty, Mrs. Montgomery closed the latch on the door with a click and then turned to me with a hatchet face which dissolved into a soft maternal smile like frost melting on winter flowers. *I know your pain*, she said. She didn't speak aloud. I heard her voice in my head.'

'Can you read my thoughts?' he asked.

'Not in the way you think.'

'Then how?'

Selena continued her story.

'Mrs. Montgomery spent the next hour telling me things I thought were superstition and folklore. She told me about magic and how I could use natural forces to improve my life. A part of me protested. What she was saying was so unbelievable and had no basis in reality, but my gut told me it was true, all of it.'

Selena looked at him and a wry smile spread on her face.

'I'm sure I looked at Mrs. Montgomery the way you're looking at me now.'

'What happened?' he asked.

'Within a month, I learned reality didn't work the way I thought it did.'

'Is this one of those I could tell you, but then I'd have to kill you type of thing?' he asked.

'Let's walk home.'

'It's quite a distance, what if it rains?' he said, looking at the sky which was milky grey like a white t-shirt which had been washed a hundred times.

'It won't,' said Selena.

*

It was nearing evening when they arrived at the cottage. The sky's edges had darkened into deep charcoal and at its centre, a ceiling of sapphire held its lustre in the day's dying moments. He'd enjoyed the walk, seeing the countryside in its bright splendour and not the eerie shapes from the night before. Despite the lateness of the year, the place was teeming with life. There were foxes, rabbits (or hares, he couldn't tell), a badger, squirrels and at least a dozen different types of birds. Selena was able to name each one in English and German. This filled him with wonder, and he recalled days from Julia's childhood when they'd go on nature walks, and he'd do the best he could to name things. Selena remarked on his memory and told him how she would occasionally travel into his thoughts when he was receptive to her.

'You were receptive to me the first time we met, you didn't even know it yourself, but I could see you shining out to me like a lighthouse.'

'Why did you ...'

'You were lost.'

'I wasn't lost,' he said, 'what do you mean lost?'

Selena was about to reply when something in her demeanour changed abruptly. She stopped and listened, and then told him to hurry.

They made good time, getting to the cottage soon afterward. As they approached the door, they heard soft breathing followed by the plaintive call of a distressed animal.

In the alcove of the door, a fawn lay curled in a delicate swirl of mottled fragility. Selena moved towards the animal and crouched down beside it. She lay her hands on its body before gently picking it up and walking through the door, which appeared to open of its own accord. He followed them into the front room where Selena placed the fawn on a broad, fat, plush chair. Tom was about to speak, but Selena raised her hand and made a pinching motion with her fingers. Before he could speak, he felt his lips be pressed together. The fawn lay with its legs tucked under its body. Its head was upright, and its eyes were bright and alert. Its chest rose and fell in a soft, regular rhythm. Selena whispered something in its ear. She stood up and turned towards the door. She took Tom's hand and led him gently from the room and closed the door quietly behind them. She didn't speak until they got into the kitchen.

'Sometimes animals come here.'

'Is it hurt?'

'It needs to rest.'

'Do you know what's wrong with it?'

'It became separated from its mother, a hunter probably …'

'Is the mother dead?'

'It's illegal to kill females with young. The penalties are severe, and they are enforced. It's likely the hunter was trying to shoot a buck or perhaps another animal when the fawn's mother got scared and ran. The fawn must have lost her scent'.

'And it came here?'

'Don't think about it too much,' she said, 'it's not something you could understand, even if I explained it to you.'

Her voice was kind, there was nothing patronising about her comment. He smiled and nodded. She then moved close to him and with a grave expression told him if he ever encountered an animal in the house, even a potentially dangerous animal, he wasn't to show any fear or aggression. If he respected its space, it wouldn't harm him.

'They don't occupy the same world we do. Their way of life is impossible to comprehend. They do their best not to intrude into our world, it's a pity we don't do the same.'

'That would explain Paddock,' said Tom.

'Black cats were especially revered by the Egyptians, but in the Middle Ages, they became associated with witches and perceptions of evil. It was entirely down to their nocturnal nature and colour. I don't need to tell you that neither cats nor witches are evil.'

Later, in the pale moony glow, he awoke with the familiar urge to go to the bathroom. Selena slept in a deep and breathy peace beside him. The first time they'd shared a bed, he'd noticed how soundly she'd slept. It was as if nothing could wake her. He envied her ability to dismiss the cares of the day in restful sleep.

He lay in bed momentarily thinking if he ignored the discomfort, he'd fall back asleep, but it was a game he rarely won. Conceding defeat, he stepped into the corridor adjoining the bedroom, standing naked in the lattice of light and shadow, before making his way to the bathroom. Once finished, he stepped back into the corridor, only to find the fawn standing at the bedroom door. It startled him, but he didn't make a sound. A small orb of reflected light dotted the upper corners of the fawn's eyes. It watched at him with a stillness only known to wild creatures. He marvelled at its perfect beauty, the shape of its head, its spindly, knotted legs, the hollow of its ears and the plush sheen of its nose. He sensed both its vulnerability and serenity and began to think how rare this was, not just in his life but in any human life, to have such an encounter. He half expected the animal to speak and, inhaling deeply through his nose, opened himself to the possibility. When it remained silent and still, he stepped back slowly, wondering what to do next.

He looked to his right down the corridor, where there was another bedroom. He would sleep there and took a slow pace forward. The fawn stepped towards him, maintaining their closeness. He paused and when the fawn didn't move, he crouched down and waited. After a few seconds, the fawn moved towards him. It bowed its head, stretched its legs, and then rested its snout on his knee. He felt the cold wetness and instinctively reached behind the fawn's ear and scratched it gently. The animal's eyes closed, and its soft breath warmed his skin.

He didn't know how long he spent with the fawn, or if he was even conscious the entire time. The moment passed in what felt like an instant, but when he noticed the first threads of dawn appearing through the window, he knew it had been much longer. Soon after the first inklings of sunrise, the fawn awoke and with a vigorous shake stirred itself into life. He stood up, expecting his muscles to protest wildly for having not moved, but when he stretched the length of his body, a great surge of wellness moved through him like he'd had the best night's rest of his life. The fawn nudged him with its nose and skipped down the corridor and into the rest of the house. He knew what it meant and followed the small animal to the front door, where he grasped the handle and opened it. A rush of morning air burst in and he braced. It had the shocking effect of a cold shower but was also invigorating. The fawn stepped into the new day and made its way down the driveway where its mother was waiting. He closed the door and went back inside. Climbing into bed beside Selena, a deep feeling of peace washed over him. Something had been lifted.

'You're cold,' said Selena, sleepily.

He closed his eyes and for a moment felt as good as he'd ever felt. He didn't tell her about the fawn, he assumed she knew already. Even had he opened his eyes, he wouldn't have seen her contented smile.

*

On the first evening, they walked to the Gothic Quarter. Barcelona had, as it turned out, been inspired, hinting at the adage that nothing is ever entirely random. It was deliciously warm, and the city was abuzz with activity. People danced in public spaces, and the entire arena of human interaction was suffused with youthful energy. Years were mere moments, and something kinetic hung in the space between the ricocheting tumult of voices. Down a labyrinth of narrow streets recessed with darkness and reverberating with a billion words uttered down the ages, Selena moved like smoke. He did his best to keep up.

*Would it be tonight*, he wondered, or would she stretch it out to take in the available time? Did it really matter when it happened?

By now he knew she could read or at least sense his thoughts, but he had learned to scatter them like seeds, whereby she may not get to his immediate thoughts immediately. Whatever fragment of his soul she was following now, she wasn't giving anything away. She had told him at the hotel she knew a place where they could enjoy some tapas and wine away from the crowds.

'Why did you run?' he asked once they were sitting.

'Why did you follow?'

He puffed out his cheeks. Beads of sweat necklaced the line of his hair, and he took a napkin from his pocket and wiped them away.

'I can't read your mind,' said Selena, abruptly.

'No, you talk to animals and cast spells on people.'

'It's not what you think it is.'

He leaned across the table. Selena reciprocated.

'Tell me the truth,' he said, 'if this is it for us, I want to know what the last five years have meant. I want to know why I've had to keep this secret to the point it's almost driven me out of my mind.'

'Your wife knows about us, if that's what you mean,' said Selena, coldly.

'It's been hard to bear at times.'

'Don't play the martyr,' said Selena dismissively, 'it doesn't suit you.'

'I wasn't …'

'I know, I'm sorry.'

The tapas bar they sat in was busy. People moved in and out along the narrow central space and music drifted in from the street, and yet, they appeared to be cocooned in a space away from everything and everyone. When they spoke, they could hear one another perfectly. There could be no misunderstanding, not at this point.

'I killed Casey Southern,' said Selena, 'and have been trying to make amends ever since.'

'The girl who bullied you in school.'

'I never finished the story.'

'I'd forgotten about it.'

He was telling the truth.

'My teacher, Mrs. Montgomery, taught me how to communicate with the world which surrounds the one we occupy.'

He was looking at her quizzically, but without scepticism.

'She'd been there during the Salem trials. She hanged for nothing more than being different. Thankfully, there were others who escaped and managed to resurrect her spirit. Since then, she moves from body to body through time, helping mostly women and keeping the group's way of life alive.'

'How do you expect me to believe that?' asked Tom.

'She taught me how to use breath to heal myself and how I could extend that to all living things. She showed me how to channel my thoughts into energy and manifest it in action. She said once I became open to the countless possibilities available to me, I'd see the world as it really was.'

'Did you?'

'Yes, but before I truly understood, I lost control of my feelings. I was consumed by revenge, and I directed every negative thought and emotion I had towards Casey Southern. By then, I could concentrate on a single thought for as long as I needed, and I wished for her death. After a while, it came to pass.'

'Are you going to tell me you cursed her?'

'She was the field hockey team captain. At the start of the year, I took the place of one of her friends. The bullying had begun there, I think. She took a dislike to me from the off. Anyway, you know about that.'

A waiter came to the table, interrupting Selena's story. They ordered two glasses of wine, staying in silent expectation until they arrived a few minutes later. Selena took a sip of her wine and carried on.

'We had a big game against our local rivals. Field hockey didn't usually attract a crowd, but this one did. I had spent the days leading up to the game focusing on Casey. It was my intention to humiliate her in front of the whole school.'

She paused to gather her thoughts.

'So, with the whole school watching, I thought I could focus my energy into causing an embarrassing failure like Casey missing an open goal and our team losing the match or her getting sent off. What I didn't know was I only had the illusion of control and when the moment came, something else was working through me, something evil, something my carelessness had allowed through from the surrounding world.'

'An evil spirit?'

'Something like that,' said Selena.

'So, what happened?'

'Casey had broken through the defence and was making a clear run for goal. I imagined her slipping just as she was about to score, followed by the whole school gasping in astonishment before bursting into collective laughter. Instead of slipping, she stumbled and fell forward and landed heavily on her neck. The ground was firm, and everyone present heard the snap. The opposition goalie was the first to see her, and she began to scream wildly as if terrified beyond belief. When I got there and saw Casey's contorted face, her eyes fixed at me in eternal blame, I knew I'd be paying for her death for the rest of my life.'

'It was an accident. I don't believe you caused it.'

'I don't care what you believe,' said Selena, gently, 'I know I did. It doesn't matter what anyone else thinks.'

He began to think about the fawn, about how it had looked at him before leaving the cottage. A realisation was coming over him.

'The baby.'

She nodded, tears were forming in her eyes, and soon a few had rolled in big drops down her cheeks.

'A life for a life, it's why the fawn came to my home and revealed itself to you.'

'I don't understand. I thought you said animals often came to your home.'

'They do, but when I carried the fawn into the house, it told me it had a message for you.'

'I didn't get a message. I mean, how would I?'

'You did,' said Selena, 'think about the time you spent alone with it, it's there, I promise you.'

'I only opened the door for it, its mother was waiting.'

'I'm sure there's more.'

He had the faraway look of someone lost in a daydream. He was remembering with precise clarity the distant afternoon where he'd made an impossible choice. He could not rescue both Julia and her sister, and had never been able to relive the events of the day until now. As he walked around his worst memory, he felt something nudging at his hand, it was the cold nose of the fawn. His daydreaming became something else, as if his mind inhabited the wrong body. His eyes were wide and staring ahead, but if you could have asked him what he was looking at, he wouldn't have been able to tell you. Selena reached across the table and took his hands. He held her fingers instinctively but without registration. It was all primal, like moving to a source of food or light. She rolled his wedding ring between her thumb and forefinger, and with her other hand tapped on the table's hard surface. A rhythm was established, and it punctuated the words she repeated over and over to him.

'Go back to your wife, be a better husband.'

She let go of his hands and stood up, her dress now white and wispy swirled about her like flames of ice. Her hair was longer and had a twist in it. She put on a pair of sunglasses and stepped out into the street. Before she left, she kissed him softly on the cheek and whispered something in his ear.

Twenty minutes later, the waiter brought the bill, and he paid it. He left the bar and made his way back to the hotel. He spent the night chasing a memory he couldn't catch before falling into a twilight doze, which was broken by the orange wisps of dawn. He rose in the morning coolness and took a long shower.

After breakfast, he packed his suitcase and left the hotel, returning to the Gothic Quarter. The city was already alive in the bright morning sun and tracing a route he somehow knew, he entered the little shop he'd noticed the night before and bought his wife a gift. He knew it would be perfect. He then walked to a nearby coffee shop and asked the young couple sitting at the table next to him what hotel they were staying in. They told him they had just arrived and had intended to stay in a hostel as they didn't have a lot of money. He handed them the key to his room; told them it was paid up for four more nights, and they were welcome to use it if they wanted. They accepted without hesitation. He smiled at them and before leaving paid their bill.

Later, as the plane to Dublin trundled on the runway, threads of autumnal light burst riotously into the cabin. He sat back, closed his eyes and fell into a soothing and lasting sleep. In his dreams, he walked through a dense wood with his wife and daughters. As they travelled deeper into the trees, a noise startled him. He looked in the direction it had come from and saw a fawn. They stared at one another for what a long time. Instinctively, Tom took a step towards the fawn. The creature bowed its head. He took another step. The fawn lifted its head. Its nose twitched and then, with a sudden movement, it ran into the undergrowth, disappearing among the swirl of earthy colours.

# PLATYPUS XI

It was one of those July evenings, muggy and thick with the leftover heat of the day, when I made my way to the cricket ground. The sea breeze, like a cat in a sun trap, barely lifted its head and had no effect on the stuffy listlessness hanging in the heavy air. The thought of doing anything active was about as welcome as a mouth ulcer.

About a month before, Billy Clifford gave me a call while I was at home idling in the June evening. I didn't recognise the number, but thinking it might be important, or at least interesting, I answered.

'Psycho,' said a voice which was at once familiar and remote, like an echo in a dream.

'Billy, it's been a while.'

'Indeed, it has. Keeping well?'

'Can't complain.'

'Sure, who'd listen?' said Billy, chuckling to himself.

Though I hadn't spoken to Billy in almost a decade, the conversation was a copy of many others I'd had with him. Billy's jocular, upbeat voice was the same.

'All well with you?' I asked.

'Never better.'

There was a short silence. I couldn't tell what Billy was thinking, but I was appreciating a fond reminisce of long-gone days.

'Are you looking for me to play cricket?' I said.

'Now, why would think that?'

'Just a hunch.'

'I'm on a bit of a mission, to be honest,' said Billy, 'are you free on July 17th?'

'What day of the week is that?'

'A Wednesday,' said Billy with the prepared brevity of someone who had been asked the same question more than once.

'Probably, can't say for sure, but yeah. What's the occasion?'

'A Platypus match, taverners, are you interested?'

I hadn't played cricket in almost seven years and became momentarily ambivalent about dusting down my whites and pulling on my spikes.

'Sure, you can let me know in a week or two if you want. No rush, but I'll need an answer by the end of next week.'

I mulled it over for a few seconds. *What the heck*, I thought, *it could be fun*.

'Pencil me in,' I said.

'Grand, will do.'

'Why are you fixing a match now, what's the occasion?' I asked.

'Ah, come on, Psycho, it's ten years since we won the cup, and I thought it might be nice to get the team back together.'

A decade before, Billy was captain of a much unfancied cupwinning team. We were a rag ball outfit of former senior players well past their best, together with some journeymen and the obligatory couple of youngsters rising through the ranks. What we lacked in ability, we made up for with a curious mix of bloody-mindedness and luck. That and what Billy called *camaraderie*, though he was probably the only one to think so. I always thought the team dynamic was more like a group of criminals.

'Ten years,' I said, recognizing the truth of how quickly time passes.

'Yep, seems like yesterday, doesn't it?' said Billy.

We chatted for a little while afterward, but Billy had to go as he'd a few others to track down. Once the call finished, memories of the lads I'd not seen in years flooded through my mind.

The impact of these memories assured me how it would be good to see them again.

Billy, apart from captaining the side, was a resilient if unorthodox, middle order batsman. He had a knack for taking the most extraordinary catches. During a tetchy match in Rathmines, Billy took a catch which made us all rub our eyes in staggered bewilderment. He was at mid-wicket and Big Trev, our opening bowler, in a late spell bowled a tired long hop the batsman pulled with the force of a cannon. I was at slip and watched as Billy, belying his years, jumped with the grace of a ballet dancer and plucked this tracer-bullet from the air one-handed, rolled on the ground before standing triumphantly holding the ball aloft, beaming from ear to ear. The batsman stood there dumbfounded. It took us a moment to comprehend what had happened. We won the game, and Billy's catch was rightly lauded as the turning point. There were more than a few pints drunk that night.

Big Trev was from Manchester. He looked benign and wore thick glasses. He could go from being your best mate one moment to wanting to punch your lights out the next. It never took much to set him off, either. My one confrontation with him was enough to make a lasting impression.

Gary Lloyd, an opening batsman, was more commonly known as The Stoat. He was a serial philanderer with a huge ego and turned every conversation to either women he was chasing or himself. He had no real interest in cricket, but enjoyed the ribald fun only a group of amateur sportsmen can have. He loved attention and making suggestive comments about someone's mother or wife, or sometimes both. He made us all laugh back then, it was harmless enough. Big Trev came close to decking him on more than one occasion. Stoat was goading Big Trev about his new girlfriend. As I recall, it was Sumo and Kiff who put the brakes on the whole thing. Anyway, that was Stoat for you, a bit of a tosser, but good craic.

I saw him from time to time through work. Stoat was never a man for a serious conversation, and was unashamedly forthright about it. He'd tell me I was boring, and I'd laugh and agree. A few weeks before the match, I bumped into him at a conference. He was at the bar talking to a woman about ten years younger than him. She was hanging on his every word, laughing, and stroking his arm, that sort of thing. As I approached, I could see Stoat's eyes lift momentarily from his companion's gaze. Before I could become a third wheel in his happy twosome, he'd intercepted me, taking me to one side like an uncle at a family gathering and told me to leave him alone as he was close to sealing the deal and didn't want me acting weird and messing up his chances. I laughed and left him to it. I'd seen it all before.

The team consisted of Sumo, squat and overweight and jolly. He batted three or four and gave the ball a right thump. Never much of a man for a quick single, he was involved in more than a few run outs, laughing about it later. He was the type of guy who made sure everyone had a beer and a smoke if they wanted one. He was universally liked. He had a perpetual wheeze and I worried about his health.

Kiff was an obnoxious, wild-haired and grizzled Aussie. I know most Aussies are hard work, but Kiff was something else. He was the guy who arrived late, often hungover, and grouchy. He'd growl at everyone and tell us cricket was a waste of time. However, once he'd shaken off his curmudgeonly exterior, he was by far our best player. He'd played grade cricket in Sydney, and rumour had it he was close to playing state. He knew Shane Warne and Matty Hayden and after a few beers would tell you how he should've played test cricket. He was a maudlin drunk, but despite the rough edges, I liked him.

As if to counter Kiff's raw boorishness, there was Moxy. Moxy was a bookish, mild-mannered Kiwi who worked in the Natural History Museum. He was tall and a little stiff, and might have been more content living in a large house in the early part of the Nineteenth Century. Kiff and Stoat would slag him mercilessly, but Moxy would never rise to their bait. Kiff and Moxy never travelled in the same car to away games. In fact, there was an order about who travelled with whom. I lived on the other side of the city and usually travelled to all matches alone. I was a bit of an outsider. This suited me as it gave me the kind of detachment I needed from the group.

Des was the only former teammate I knew who would not be taking part in the match. Ten months after our cup win, he passed away. He'd been battling cancer for three years and was determined to play one final season. The fact we'd won the cup was icing on the cake. On the raspy May afternoon almost ten years before, when Stoat called to tell me Des was gone, it didn't mean a whole lot to me. Des was my teammate, but he was their friend, and in the following years I was mindful of their loss and how a stillness would descend whenever his name got mentioned. Des had two young kids then.

Billy had told me they'd be coming to the match.

The Platypus name and its oddly cross-cultural motto *Tous 4 Un* and *Un 4 Tous* came from an incident in Melbourne Zoo the winter before our cup triumph. Billy and his wife had visited Australia and Billy, a keen photographer, was intent on snapping a few wildlife pics. He spent two hours waiting patiently for a duck-billed platypus to emerge from its den, but to no avail. This didn't bother him. He was sanguine about it, but as the story goes, a fat and sweaty Frenchman accused the zoo of not actually having a platypus and then proceeded to cause a scene by swearing at all in sundry in French. Billy's wife, a French teacher, managed to calm the man down. It wasn't much of a story, but to hear Billy tell it was a lot of fun. Billy was a proper raconteur with terrific comic timing and an incredible ability to mimic. His fat, sweaty Frenchman was Inspector Clouseau and Rene Artois rolled into one. I think it was this relaxed manner and leadership which contributed greatly to our success, modest as it was.

I only played another year with the club before returning to my original club. My final summer with the team was filled with nostalgia. Most of this was down to Des' death, the rest down to the cup run. We would take turns delivering anecdotes about great shots and catches, wickets taken and near heroic defiance in the face of certain defeat. We all knew the reality was a very minor victory in a very minor sport in a very minor country, but in the telling, in the group's sanctity, we were giants. I loved to hear the events and how we got our nicknames. I was called Psycho or, more fully, *Suddenly Psychotic* because I would regularly and vehemently protest umpiring decisions.

*That time in Railway when Psycho bowled a beamer and the umpire threatened to have him expelled from the game and Psycho said it slipped and then, two balls later, he did it again.*

*It was raining, it did slip.*

*It didn't slip, you fucking liar. You fucked it at the cunt's head. Fucking A Psycho. FUCK-ING A, man.*

*Or the time in The Brook when he ripped through the top-order. Had a hot date that night?*

*You know it.*

*Yeah, with Big Trev's mot.*

*You watch it Stoat, or I'll break your stupid pointy face.*

*Your bird can sit on my pointy face.*

*Easy Trev, he's just winding you up.*

\*

Driving into the club for the first time in almost ten years was eerie. I couldn't tell if it was real or a stunningly convincing simulation. The heat was heavy in a humid, relentless way, and I was tired from work and life in general. This match was inconvenient for a few reasons, mostly location and day. I knew there'd be a few jars after the game down in O'Leary's, so I'd have to leave the car and get a DART home and collect it the next day. Mid-week was a pain in the arse, but I dismissed my objections and admonished myself for thinking the way a middle-aged, set-in-his-ways man would. But I was middle-aged and set in my ways. I got out of my car and opened the boot and grabbed my bag and bat.

'You're not going to need that.'

It was Sumo. He looked heavier than when I'd last seen him. His face was rounder and redder, and his eyes were set back behind the chubbiness of his cheeks. He offered his hand. I shook it warmly. He offered me a smoke.

'I quit,' I said.

'Jaysus, everyone I know has quit,' he said, 'am I going to die as the team's last smoker?'

I chuckled at his gallows humour.

'How did you quit?'

'It was easy,' I said, 'I had a kid.'

'Of course, Stoat told me, a boy?'

'A girl, Olivia.'

Sumo laughed loudly, a proper belly laugh which filled the warm air and carried out into the open spaces.

'It was a fifty-fifty chance,' he said, 'how old is she now?'

'Eight, almost nine.'

'That's great.'

'I heard you got married,' I said.

'Yeah, two years ago, to Carly, she's American,' said Sumo and then added, grabbing his midriff, 'I definitely fit in there.'

We laughed.

'Good to see you, mate,' I said.

'Good to see you,' he said in turn.

We walked slowly to the clubhouse, and he told me about how his decade had gone. It was mostly trivial stuff, but talking to Sumo had the soothing quality of a zen garden. As we got near, I could see Billy. He'd put on a bit of weight too and still had the same Beatlesque haircut which made him look younger than he was. It was only when I got close enough to see his face, I saw how time had etched lines and age in his skin. It was like stretched paper. Only his eyes retained their flickering lust for life as they shifted in tiny movements, taking in all the available light.

'You and Trev will be opening,' said Billy, getting straight to business, 'sort it out between yourselves as to who'll take the first over.'

It had been decided before the game which team would bat first. Our opposition were an amalgam of various other local clubs, and I recognised a few faces from yesteryear. There were waves and gestures exchanged.

'I haven't bowled in years, Billy, I'll put my back out.'

'I doubt it, Psycho, you look as fit as a butcher's dog. Have you lost weight?'

'A little,' I said, coyly.

'That's what married life will do for you,' said Billy.

'Hasn't done that for me,' said Sumo.

We laughed.

Gathered in the dressing room were Billy, myself, Sumo and Big Trev, who was in one of his less approachable moods. Kiff arrived soon after. He looked the same. He'd been shattered by booze and hard living in his thirties so now, in his forties, the only difference was a harder face and grouchier mood. He sat near Big Trev. The two of them snarled at one-another. Trev called Kiff a wanker and Kiff called Trev a cunt, and after that, they shook hands and set about getting ready to play. Big Trev looked up from his gear bag. His eyes fixed on me.

'Do you want first over?'

I shook my head. Trev nodded.

Billy's phone beeped, and then a few seconds later beeped again.

'Stoat is running late and Moxy says he can't make it.'

'Fucking kiwis can't fucking rely on them for fuck all,' spat Kiff.

'Not a problem,' said Billy, 'I expected a cry-off or two, so a few lads from the oppo will join us.'

'Some things never change,' said Sumo.

The two youngsters who were part of the cup run a decade before were now in their mid-twenties and had each politely declined Billy's invitation to take part. It was just as well, since both were accomplished players and would struggle to gain any value from the kind of match we would play.

We spent a few minutes talking about this and that. No one mentioned Des or how his wife and kids had not turned up.

About five minutes before we were due to start, Stoat arrived with a flourish. He swung his BMW into the carpark, blaring insipid RNB and honking his horn. The small crowd of spectators (mostly elderly club members) turned collectively like a group of meerkats. Stoat stepped from his car with a swagger. He was wearing a tailored suit and shades and the smug, arrogant grin we all knew well.

'I will be with you knobheads as soon as I'm ready.'

'Get yerself out her quick smart,' said Big Trev, 'we're a man light in the field.'

'Fielding is so boring,' said Stoat dismissively.

'A kick up the arse will be boring if you don't get a move on.'

Ten minutes later, Stoat sauntered onto the field, wearing the same shades and smug grin. I was preparing to bowl and even though this match was non-competitive, I was apprehensive. I had a reputation for being either excellent or dismal depending on the day, and I was wondering which version of me was about to turn up. As it happened, I was middling-fair. The first ball I bowled in years found a length and beat the batsman.

'Quality stuff, Psycho,' said Billy, clapping enthusiastically.

'That will keep the punters at Uttoxeter interested,' said Stoat. By now, his hands were down the front of his trousers. I knew he was bored to death.

Other than himself, Stoat's other great interest was horse racing. He knew a lot about it and enjoyed making bets. I think he won a fair bit. That said, he never shared a tip. In the Platypus glory days, Stoat's way of relieving the boredom which only fielding and perhaps a protestant service could induce, was to do a rambling and often entertaining commentary of an imaginary horse race. The runners often had predictable but funny names like Mucky Trout or Yer Ma, as in 'Sumo is on Yer Ma, the going is good to firm, though with this kind of a weight handicap it's likely she won't go the distance ...' and so on. This time he was naming various courses.

'Doncaster.'

'Ludlow.'

'Ffos Las.'

'Southwell.'

'Wincanton.'

'Shut up you pillock,' said Big Trev as Stoat persisted uttering inanities, 'you're breaking my concentration.'

'Your bird's face is breaking my concentration,' said Stoat.

Big Trev threw the ball at him hard and glowered for a good ten seconds. The ball missed Stoat's head by inches. The racing commentary stopped.

The game progressed in a somewhat desultory manner. Enthusiasm at the outset gave way to the realisation the game itself was not a great idea and what we should have done was meet for a meal or pints. Over the years, Billy tried to arrange such an outing, but for one reason or another it never came to be. He met with Stoat and Kiff and Sumo on a semi-regular basis as they all lived near one-another and frequented the same places. Billy figured out the only way to bring me, Big Trev and Moxy into the fold was to endure the crack of leather on willow for a couple of hours. As we walked off the field between innings, I could see a growing tiredness in everyone, as if we were battle-weary and aware of death's presence like an encroaching storm. As we sat in the dressing room, I mentioned Des. I'd no idea why; it just came out. Billy was the first to speak, and I was grateful he did.

'He'd have enjoyed this.'

'You said his wife and kids were coming.'

'I said they might,' retorted Billy, there was an edge to his voice.

'I don't blame them,' said Stoat, 'don't know why I bothered myself.'

There was nothing more after that. Stoat and Sumo went out to bat and after them Kiff, Billy, me, a few others and finally Big Trev.

We won the game, but it meant nothing. The light was barely good enough to play, even at the gentle pace we were going. A line of gold split the horizon and by dusk we had showered and dressed, and most had made their way to O'Leary's. I lingered a while, realising this would likely be the final time I'd be in the ground. I'd thought the same nine years before, but this time the feeling was keener, like the edge of an old blade newly whetted. Billy was the last to emerge into the half-light.

'Are you going to O'Leary's?'

I nodded.

'I'll see you down there,' said Billy, going to his car.

I opened the boot of my car and rather than throw my gear into it as I would have in earlier times, I placed it in with the gentleness of someone laying an infant in its cot. The night closed in, and stars rose in the growing cool. I closed the boot with a thunk and made my way through the leafy opulence of Sandymount to the relative civility of O'Leary's.

*

The pub wasn't exactly as I remembered it. It felt smaller with lower ceilings and the light was less bright. After jostling through the space to where the lads had assembled, I spent a few minutes looking at the memorabilia on the walls before joining them. O'Leary's and the club had a long history, and its walls were adorned with photos of various teams, both great and mediocre, through the years.

'It's over there,' said Billy, pointing to a spot near the bar.

I wasn't sure what he meant at first, but soon realised what he was pointing to. I nodded, and an uncharacteristic well of sentimentality began to rise within me. I stood before the photo and couldn't help but feel both connected and disconnected in the moment. I caught my face reflected in the frame and imagined I was looking at a stranger. The photo was taken immediately after we'd won the cup. We were all grinning ear-to-ear, holding bottles of beer arms draped over one-another in both victory and fellowship. The cup was, truth be told, insignificant and small. Despite this, it stood proudly in the centre of the line-up. Observing the photo, I recalled how, after the final, we'd returned to

O'Leary's where Davy, the head barman, filled the cup with all manner of booze.

*The trick is to keep clear spirits with clear spirits and dark spirits with dark. Never mix the two.*

The first mouthful I took tasted mostly of tequila and peach schnapps. It was like swallowing perfumed dish soap. The next fill tasted mostly of brandy and rum. I don't remember taking a third mouthful.

As I reminisced, Kiff, who was in a warmly benign mood, gave me a chummy pinch on the shoulder. He pushed his head past mine and looked at the photo.

'Handsome fuckers, except for Moxy, he looks like a giraffe's dick.'

'Do you want a drink?' I said.

Kiff took a mouthful from his glass.

'Yeah, why not.'

We moved to the bar and after a bit of gentle elbowing took a space. I ordered a couple of beers.

'Do you remember the last time we had a drink in this place?' said Kiff.

I didn't know how to answer the question. Kiff was a former teammate, not a mate and yet, the question was couched in the language of friendship.

'The cup final?' I said.

'Yep, we drank Malibu and blackcurrant.'

I'd no recollection of the event, and Malibu and blackcurrant didn't seem like something either of us would drink.

'Pints of Malibu and blackcurrant,' said Kiff, seeming to savour the memory.

The barman arrived with our drinks. Kiff took his.

'Cheers, mate,' he said, offering his glass.

'Cheers,' I said, tapping my glass onto his.

'You heard Big Trev and his wife split up?'

'I didn't even know he was married,' I said.

'Yep, about six months ago. Rumour has it he hit her but keep it under your hat.'

The lads were gathered around a large table and things were loud and animated. Stoat held court with all the bluster of a right-wing politician, but no one was listening. Big Trev, Billy and Sumo were talking among themselves and occasionally giving Stoat a tacit nod. It was the lads from the opposition who'd joined us who were having their ears bent by Stoat's mix of casual misogyny and purposeful narcissism.

'He's a bit full on,' said one an opposition lad, 'is he always like this?'

'He's usually not this bad, but he's had a few, means no harm' said Kiff

'It's hard to know what he means,' I said.

'He needs to change the record, it was a laugh back in the day, but it's just bullshit now,' said Big Trev loudly.

Stoat must have heard him because he paused and looked at Big Trev.

'Is there a problem?' said Big Trev.

Billy distracted Trev, who was starting to adopt a menacing look. Trev smiled a broad, toothy smile and resumed his chat with Billy and Sumo. After a while, the conversation opened up and Stoat's pronouncements were relegated to background noise. Billy retold the platypus tale to the great enjoyment of all, especially the opposition lads. Stoat, having the table's attention, was scrolling through his phone.

We traded anecdotes over a couple of drinks. The lads ribbed me about leaving the club, but it was in good spirits.

'You were never truly one of us,' said Billy, 'never a disciple.'

'Honorary,' said Big Trev.

'For certain,' said Billy, 'but never let it be said that any one of us is not a platypus. Tous 4 Un.'

We raised our glasses and tipped them together with a tinkling chime.

'Best moments,' said Billy, 'the highlight reel. Who's first?'

'Your catch in Leinster,' said Sumo.

There was a chorus of agreement, even after all these years, it had to be the single most amazing moment of our cricketing careers.

'Psycho's bouncer against Clontarf,' said Billy, 'the one that dropped that prick, what's his name?'

'Nearly took the fucker's head off.'

'What was his name?' said Billy.

I gave him the answer and a consensus agreed the named individual was indeed a prick.

A lounge girl was in the process of clearing the glasses from our table and had to pass by Stoat to get to the top part of it. As she squeezed past him, Big Trev looked at her and then nodded to Stoat.

'You'd want to watch him, love, he's on the sex offender's register. Got an eye for girls your age, and younger. Did time in The Joy, so he did.'

The girl shrunk and instinctively looked at Stoat. She smiled awkwardly. Her face blanched. Stoat pushed his chair back and gave her plenty of space. She left quickly, carrying as many glasses as she could. An air of perfect stillness descended on the group as Big Trev and Stoat stared at one another. The silence escalated and hung in the air like a bad smell. Billy's eyes darted between Stoat and Big Trev. The opposition lads got up, not wanting any part of it. The stillness, now as tense as a coiled snake, lingered a little longer until Kiff broke in.

'Best one yet, Trev. Fucking A, man.'

A smirk broke out on Stoat's face, and soon Big Trev followed.

'Got to admit he got you fucking good,' said Kiff.

Stoat leaned across the table and offered his hand to Big Trev. They shook and Billy took a deep breath as if he'd surfaced from a deep dive.

'Of course, it's only a matter of time before he's actually on the sex offenders list,' said Sumo.

As things wound down and the evening came to its natural conclusion, a sombre feeling moved among the group like fog through a street. Billy must have sensed that everyone was about ready to leave and stood up.

'The best platypus moment for me was Des' fifty in the cup semi. Stand up lads.'

We stood in unison, quiet and serious, as if we were at a funeral.

'To Des and other absent friends,' said Billy, raising his glass.

We repeated what he'd said and raised our glasses and after downing whatever remained in them, we gathered coats and phones and other sundries and two minutes after the toast were outside in the cool July night. The moon was big over the bay and despite the hour, the last traces of light could be seen stretching into the darkness.

'See you in another ten years,' said Billy, shaking my hand. Sumo, Big Trev and Stoat expressed similar sentiments and even though I knew I was over the limit, I felt as sober as a judge. Kiff, being Kiff, called us a bunch of fuckers and wandered off into the night.

I drove home slowly and without incident. I decided to sleep in the spare room. It seemed appropriate to do so.

I didn't hear from anyone for about a month when my phone rang one Saturday afternoon.

It was Stoat.

'Sumo had a heart attack yesterday,' he said.

'Is he alright?'

'He's dead.'

I didn't know what to say.

'That's two down,' said Stoat.

'How old was he?'

'He was only fifty.'

We exchanged a few banalities before hanging up. It occurred to me that in the cup final, Des had been dismissed first, followed by Sumo. I know it was just a coincidence, but I ran through the order of who lost their wickets. I knew in time there'd be three of us gone, then four, five and so on. This gave me pause, but I didn't dwell upon it. I thought of all the matches

I'd played over the years and how encroaching rain clouds would threaten to end them. I then thought about how many were lost to rain.

The clouds were gathering in their slow, inevitable way, but in my heart, I believed there was still some sunlight left in the day. I reckoned we might get another few matches in before it got too dark to play.

# THE OCCULTING LIGHT

I made it to St. Augustine Lighthouse in late July. I was a little behind schedule, but still within safe margins if I were to avoid the worst of hurricane season. I aimed to finish at Key West Lighthouse sometime in August but was now revising my plan for an early-mid September finish. Diane, my editor, was beginning to fray around the edges as I asked to extend deadlines.

She had no particular interest in the project and made her feelings explicitly clear to me at our first meeting. She didn't understand why I was wasting the publisher's money on what she called a *pointless and costly adventure.*

'There are lots of books on North American lighthouses', she said to me, 'what do you want to write which hasn't already been written?'

I'd known a lot of hardheaded editors over the years, but my relationship with Diane was more than butting heads, it was stormy. I decided she was trying to prove herself. She had come to the publishing house with a stellar reputation, and the weight of expectation hung heavily on her. When I first met her, she sat behind a neat desk which was all angles and edges. The office we sat in had been where, thirty years before, I had signed my first contract. I told her the story by way of introduction. She said it was a cute story.

The publisher, perhaps for fun, perhaps by way of initiation, decided to put Diane on a project I'd been mulling for a long time. Ordinarily, I'd have worked with my regular editor, Ben

Atwell, but as this project took my writing in a new direction, the publisher felt Diane might help me see things in a whole new light. I asked him if he had any particular viewpoint on what I wanted to do. His words were succinct, as ever.

'Do what you like, Walt, I'm sure it'll sell.'

We both knew I'd made him enough money over the years.

Diane cut her teeth at a university press in California before moving into mainstream publishing. I was sure she was sick of dealing with old men with old ideas. Academic texts were her speciality. Her desire was to work with fiction.

I was not writing a fiction book this time round. Diane was busy and techy and had a strange way of looking at the world. Her eyes moved like a wading bird searching the shallows for fish.

Despite our differences, I liked her straight away, even if she didn't care for me or what I had to say. She reminded me of my daughter, Ellen. Diane was an old head on young shoulders, you could spot it a mile off. I can't tell you the number of times teachers and sports coaches had said the same about Ellen, though never to me.

Diane held up a copy of *The Light List III, Atlantic Coast, Little River, South Carolina to Econfina River, Florida.* She pushed her glasses up the ridge of her nose.

'You write fiction, you're good at it. Why do you want to write about old, largely unoccupied buildings which no-one has a use for anymore?'

I wanted to correct her and tell her about the working lighthouses along the Atlantic coast but decided to humour her instead, she'd have to read about it all soon enough.

'I feel like doing it,' I said, 'an old man's indulgence.'

I could sense she wanted to roll her eyes. She accused me of being reckless with her new employer's money. I smirked. She did not.

'You have Irish heritage, don't you?'

She frowned. Her mood was all business.

'I don't think that Mc in your surname is Native American.'

'What's your point?'

'Minot's Ledge is a lighthouse just south of Boston. It's in Cohasset Harbor, about a mile offshore. In October 1849, a ship named the St. John hit the rocks and all ninety-nine Irish immigrants on board drowned within view of their new home. Don't you think that's an interesting story?'

'It's fascinating.'

'There's no need for sarcasm,' I said.

'You're right, so why don't you write a historical account of it?'

'Because the scope isn't broad enough, I want to focus on more than one maritime tragedy that's played out on the Atlantic coast.'

She acknowledged I had the publisher's blessing and how she didn't necessarily look forward to working with me on the project.

I asked her if the publisher had given her any direction or discretion. She said, no, all she'd been told was to help me write my book.

'I won't make it difficult for you,' I said reassuringly.

The idea was simple. I would begin with Portland Head Light in Maine and work my way down the coast to Florida. I had planned a route, a rough time scale and made primary contact with the various people I planned on interviewing along the way. I was interested in how light keeping was often a family business, how widows often took over from their husbands and how for all the souls saved, many more were lost. Sea lore needed to be chronicled and while Diane was right about there being an abundance of books exploring the history of lighthouses along the Atlantic coast, she had no idea about other motivations I had for adding to the pile.

\*

Ellen was my daughter, though not my wife's daughter.

Let me explain.

By some quirk of fate, my third novel had been a surprising success, making the New York Times bestseller list. There was even interest from Hollywood. Described as *a taut political thriller in the style of John Le Carré*, it established me as a writer and not someone who merely wrote. It earned me an invite to The White House as part of one of those lip-service celebrations of the arts the elite are so fond of. Apparently, President Clinton had read my book and the premise (a Russian plant posing as VP) had amused him.

I stood in The Grand Foyer, feeling like an impostor. I'd struck it lucky with a potboiler, and now I was rubbing shoulders with some serious literary heavyweights like Updike, Irving and Toni Morrison. I was a wayfarer on the outskirts of any conversation, the only question a fellow writer asked me was why I was there alone. I explained my wife was a schoolteacher and couldn't drop everything midweek and, besides, we had two kids, so the logistics were much easier if I attended alone. They gave me a look dripping with pity and walked away. Clinton passed through the room. He shook hands and shared small talk with the high-ranking guests. I tried to move closer to the action but was re-buffed, so I took two glasses of champagne from a passing wait-er and slipped into the shadows.

I was relatively late to the writing game. I was in my early for-ties. Like many writers, I'd spent most of my life teaching Eng-lish by day and writing by night. I'd never expected any success, so when it came, I mistakenly thought I'd be able to take it in my stride, but the years of pent-up frustration at my lack of ac-knowledgement made me feel a little superior and cocky, espe-cially towards those who'd doubted me in the early days. After my second novel hit the bookstores, I'd lie in bed writing sneer-ing letters in my head to gym teachers who'd said I'd amount to nothing and stuffy editors who'd rejected me.

It was this admission which led to an encounter in a decorative bathroom with the tipsy wife of a senator. She joined me in the shadows as the President uttered platitudes and shook hands with the suck-ups.

'I hate this part,' she said, 'it's such a pageant.'

We guzzled champagne and I told her my story. Soon afterward, she was taking my hand and telling me to follow. All I could think the whole time was whether her husband was a democrat or a republican. Back then, it was okay to mingle with the opposition.

And so it would come to pass, I'd watch my daughter grow up and live the life I couldn't give her. About ten weeks after the party, the senator's wife contacted me under the auspices of her 'book club' and told me the news. I asked her if she was sure I was the father. She was. Her husband, who was fifteen years older, had recently had bypass surgery and sexual activity of all kinds had been off limits long before our White House tryst.

'You're not that attractive,' said the senator's wife, 'you were available, and I was a bit drunk.'

'How are you going to explain it to your husband?' I asked.

'He's a politician, avoiding a scandal is his skill, besides a new baby will help his re-election.'

She told me she was keeping the child and if I complained or said anything or tried to intervene, she'd ruin my career. She told me I was not needed financially or emotionally and without another option, I could do nothing but agree to these terms. At the time it looked like I'd got off lightly and for a while, I had. I carried on as normal, I wrote my books and watched my other kids grow up. All thoughts of Ellen and her mother took a back seat in my mind, until five years later. I was watching the news after dinner. There was nothing of particular interest, except a breaking story telling how a senator had collapsed during a meeting of the Judiciary Committee. At first, his name didn't register with me, but when The White House Press Secretary released a statement wishing the senator a speedy recovery and how he and his family were in the President's thoughts, it hit me hard. Ellen was four at the time, and I was grabbed by a powerful urge to connect with her.

'What is it?' asked my wife, 'you look like you've seen a ghost.'

I had to scramble a reply.

'I met him and his wife a few years ago at that thing in The White House.'

'They must have made quite an impression,' said my wife.

'They liked my book.'

I didn't sleep much that night. I needed to follow the story on T.V. The third time I got out of bed, my wife told me to sleep in the spare room.

The senator died a week later. The day after his death, his wife issued a statement thanking those who supported him. She asked people to respect the family's privacy and so on. After she'd stepped away from the cameras, a small child ran towards her. She gathered it up into her arms. This was the first time I'd seen my daughter. Her face turned to the camera, and I saw my grandmother's features there as clear as day.

*She's a Barrett,* I thought, *she'll be okay.*

From then on, I followed her life as best I could from a distance. The senator's wife ended up taking his seat. Try as I could, Ellen dipped under my radar until she was about twenty, when she rose to national prominence as one of the nation's most promising sailors. Growing up in the northeast, she'd taken to the water and, despite her young age, was tipped to take a place at the Rio Olympics. There was some nonsense in the papers about her not being worth a place, but when the team was announced in the spring, and she had made it, I was overjoyed. I immediately made plans to go to Brazil. Enough time had passed in my mind and now after years of this big secret, I felt this was an opportunity to meet her.

About a month before the games began, I almost told my wife the truth but backed out at the last minute. I needed to create a ruse, so I told her I was going to the Olympics to research an article.

'I always wanted to be in *Sports Illustrated,*' I said.

'You've never written an article in your life,' said my wife.

'I wrote a piece for *The Atlantic* ten years ago, and *The Georgia Review*.'

'Book reviews,' said my wife dismissively, 'and not good ones at that.'

'A man can change; do you want to come with me?'

My wife had grown up in Minnesota and while she enjoyed the temperate heat of North Carolina, where we lived, the humidity of summertime in Brazil was not for her and I knew it.

'What are you up to?' she said, looking at me through narrowing eyes.

I decided to keep my secret a little longer. I imagined a meaningful relationship with Ellen as part of my future. Another part of this fantasy was my wife being okay with the whole thing. It was naive. I knew deep down those things rarely worked out.

The conception of Ellen was the only time I was unfaithful to my wife. I'd had opportunities on book tours and at conferences, but the events in The White House had been enough to throw a scare into me. Instead of doing things in person, I did what most fiction writers did and wrote about characters with buried secrets and secret desires. Despite this, my paranoia never completely vanished, and I lived in constant worry that one day the truth about Ellen would surface in a way I had no control over.

\*

*St. Augustine Light was first lit in 1824, though the second lighthouse on the north end of Anastasia Island didn't come into operation until 1874. It is arguable St. Augustine lays claim to North America's oldest lighthouse, as the Spanish lit beacons here dating back to 1565.*

I looked up from my laptop and peered towards the Atlantic. It stretched to the horizon. At the shore, white surf rushed up the sand in small swells. Further out, the aquamarine blue deepened into a rich cobalt. Somewhere below my window, voices danced on the air.

Whenever I travelled, I liked to stay at The Embassy Suites if one was available. St. Augustine's Embassy Suites were about a mile walk from the lighthouse, and my room had a balcony with an unobstructed ocean view. I spent the afternoon talking to the lighthouse operators about its history. They told me stories, which I would later sift through for my chapter on the lighthouse.

I had narrowed it down to either a story about German U-Boats in World War II or a spooky story from The Civil War. I was leaning towards The Civil War story, as I'd noticed how hauntings were becoming a pattern in the narrative I was telling. This was the tenth lighthouse I'd visited on my trip.

I had started at Portland Head Light in Maine, where I'd told a story of drowned lobstermen whose ghosts were said to haunt the shallows when the fog rolled in. Next, I had moved to Boston Light on Little Brewster Island, America's second oldest working lighthouse and spent a wonderful evening with the lightkeeper, a real hoary old sea dog in the manner of Quint from *Jaws*. He told me stories of mysterious goings-on and mermaids and other such seafaring lore. I took great delight writing about that experience. After Boston Light, I travelled to Minot's Ledge and, like Diane suggested, related a tale about the ninety-nine Irish immigrants who drowned there.

Block Island Southeast Light, Rhode Island, came next. Being architecturally interesting, my chapter focused on this aspect and was free of ghosts, despite there being a supernatural tale associated with the place.

I was sending chapters to Diane, and she was returning suggestions. She was razor sharp and reminded me of the editors I'd worked with in my early days. They were real drill-sergeants and didn't let me away with anything. The pages I would email her came back covered in red lines and corrections. At first, I thought she was getting some payback, but as I analysed her ideas, I noticed her skill. She told me my latest novel was lazy and how she wouldn't allow her first significant work with the publishing house be a target for criticism.

*You have the makings of a novel here,* she wrote in an email. I agreed, but I knew it wouldn't get written.

I had expected the highpoint of my journey to be Cape Hatteras in North Carolina. I knew the place well. I'd lived in Edenton for many years and would take occasional trips to the cape. The first time I saw the lighthouse, it was late summer of 1999, just before Hurricane Floyd. I was struck by its majesty. Conical in shape and distinctively striped in black and white, it stood at an imposing 210ft and had a range of 24 nautical miles. The sea off the Outer Banks was treacherous, earning the area the nickname The Graveyard of the Atlantic. Many ships had run aground on the shifting sandbars, and without the guidance of Cape Hatteras Light, it's impossible to tell how many more ships would have been lost.

During each lighthouse visit, I negotiated and sometimes begged to see them being lit. In most cases, this was a simple and uneventful process involving the flick of a switch. It was somewhat underwhelming and didn't put me in touch with the light keepers of the nineteenth and early twentieth centuries as I'd hoped. Their task was a much more solemn and vocational one. The modern light keeper, as far as I could tell, was essentially a tour guide.

The keeper at Cape Hatteras was a difficult man who jealously guarded his duty and didn't enjoy my presence in the tower. He took a great deal of persuading but eventually agreed, albeit grudgingly, to allow me to see the light being lit. As he set it up, I asked him questions about the type of lens and the 24 nautical miles, and he grumbled and told me to go outside as he was about to turn on the light and I could find out all about it for myself.

It was spectacular. For an instant, the entire world illuminated before the beam's focus ripped open the sea's surface, producing a line of gold stretching far into the darkness. The light held like this for a time before going completely dark, only to resume its vigil a short time later. It was like an eclipse.

'Occulting light,' said the keeper who stood behind me in the hard dark. I had not noticed him arrive.

'Fifty-six seconds bright and constant per minute, four dark. Works best on nights like this.'

He said nothing more and left me to look seaward, where I thought of those who had died for lack of direction on a moonless night.


\*


The amount of red tape to secure passage to Rio was as stifling and sapping as swimming through a sea of hot jelly. Visas, vaccinations, and an independent press pass took much longer than I expected. I arrived into the thick heat of Rio after a dreadfully bumpy flight from Miami. By the time I'd got through immigration, my shirt was wet and heavy, and I needed a drink.

The hotel air-conditioning was heavenly and while I was cocooned on the island of calm I had created amid the city's chaos; I realised I had no plan about what to do next. In my mind, the process was straightforward, but in practical terms it was not.

Sailing events, including practice, took place in Marina da Gloria in Guanabara Bay. I attended them every day. It reminded me of a youthful summer I'd spent in Cape Cod. A college friend, now deceased, lived in Wellfleet. He invited a bunch of us to stay. This was in 1975 and the memory was still searingly vivid. We swam and sailed and drank beer and built bonfires on the beach. When Jaws hit the cinemas on June 20th, our relationship with the water changed. There was no such drama or danger in the marina. Large crowds of spectators viewed the proceedings from newly erected stands, and a bubbling and vibrant community grew around the event.

I watched Ellen from the achingly familiar distance I'd known all her life. I brought binoculars and watched as she pushed herself to the limits. I can't tell you how it felt to be the father of an

Olympian. My elder son was a banker, my younger, a realtor. Neither could throw a baseball, and neither could swim worth a damn.

On the fourth day I had a moment of serendipity which, like many of these moments, began with doubt and even fear.

I bumped into Ellen's mother.

'When you get back to DC, will you punch Ted Cruz on the nose for me?' I said.

'I'm no longer in the senate.'

I thought I'd made a terrible error. Her face was taut and serious and despite the heat, I felt a chill.

'But if I was, I would definitely do it,' she said finally.

I laughed. We spoke for a few minutes. I told her I wanted to see Ellen.

'I saw you two days ago, I could have approached you then, but I wanted to be sure,' she said.

'She's turned into an amazing woman,' I said.

'She has, she must have inherited her tenacity from you.'

'She looks like my grandmother,' I said, 'does she know the truth?'

'She knows her father was not her father.'

I nodded.

'I'll speak to her, she has a lot going on at the moment. There are strict rules about when she can see friends and family.'

'Even for a former senator?'

'Even for a former senator.'

We swapped numbers. The next day I got a message inviting me to a brunch at the team compound. I had been there a week and my skin felt like leather. I looked like an old satchel. My eyes were droopy and tired and every morning when I would peer at myself in the mirror, I couldn't help but think how old I was. The summer of 1975 became as distant as the moon.

Before leaving to meet Ellen, I emailed my wife and told her why I had travelled to Rio. Calling her was not an option, she'd harangue me with questions and demand answers. All this would happen while her voice remained implacably calm. It was her most potent weapon. Years of teaching and administering in the public school system had given her the ability to inflict devastation with spoken words. I had often referred to the fact while I wrote for a living, she spoke for a living. She told me once that spoken words are more honest than written ones. Spoken words, she said, were like light because they revealed the immediacy of emotion, whereas written words lurked in the darkness between the writer's intention and action.

'You have lived a life in the shadows,' she said.

My email subject line read 'from the shadows'.

Ellen's mother met me at a prearranged place. We walked from there to the compound.

'Should I be nervous?' I said.

'I'm not sure.'

'I emailed my wife. I didn't give specifics, I said I had a daughter.'

'You've kept it secret a long time, how will she take it?'

'I don't know, but I don't really care.'

'Even if it ends your marriage?'

I shrugged. My marriage hadn't been anything more than a domestic arrangement for some time.

'I don't know what your plans are with Ellen, but your timing is bad.'

'Why is that?'

'She's going to Europe to study.'

'That's great.'

'I expect she'll settle there,' continued Ellen's mother, 'she's always wanted to get away. I feel she's had enough of her American life. She speaks endlessly about whitewater kayaking in Scandinavia.'

There was distance in her words, like a sound carried across a chasm.

I wanted to ask more questions, but there was no point, I'd know soon enough.

*

After Cape Hatteras, I took in Hunting Island light near Beaufort and followed with a visit to Tybee Island light near Savannah. Both are conical lighthouses, and both have black and white daymarking, which is standard for the region along the Carolinas, Georgia and into northern Florida. Hunting Island was pleasant, if unremarkable. I had included it in my itinerary because, somehow, I had never been to Beaufort despite countless recommendations from almost everyone I knew. As soon as I arrived, I saw what I'd been missing. Huge gnarled live oaks flanked wide sleepy avenues. Spanish moss hung from their sprawling limbs like cats in the sun. Big wood-framed houses from a different era sat back off the street with a reassuring and refreshing sense of ease which permeated the entire setting.

I spent a lovely evening in the company of Beaufort's rotary club. The light keeper was a member, and he insisted I join them before we lit the bulb. As it turned out, a few of them were fans of my books and while I normally tried to stay distant from my readers, these people, who were mostly my age, were good-natured and a lot of fun. I felt like I was part of an old gang, perhaps one who'd grown up in the town, who'd spent lazy summer days and nights on Hunting Island listening to The Beach Boys, feeling the breeze brush through long hair as the sea hinted at a future which would be unceasingly bright. Something about the late 60s and 70s, despite all its challenges, projected a sense of unabashed hope. I'd seen this hope dwindle in the Reagan years, and now in the strangeness of the modern world I felt it had burned out. Among this group, however briefly and illusory, it was rekindled.

After my time with the rotary club, the lighthouse was something of an anti-climax. I promised the gang I'd write about them. Diane enjoyed the chapter. She made no changes.

As a child, I had visited Tybee Island with my parents. I had no lasting memories, just vague images. My return, over fifty years later, was something of a homecoming. So much was different, but there was enough similarity to let my feelings for the place come back like a tidal surge. I took a long slow stroll along the beach and onto the pier where I chatted to a couple of guys who were fishing. They told me they were hoping to land a few lemon sharks, but mostly only red drum and sheepshead were biting.

'Sharks are harder to catch these days,' said one of them, 'I think it's the boats and submarines. It screws up their senses, and they get lost.'

The lighthouse is on the island's north point, where the Savannah River enters the sea. Like a lot of lighthouses, it had a troubled history. The first lighthouse was built in 1736 but was later felled by a storm in 1741. A brick tower was built thereafter, and it lasted until 1862 when Confederate forces burned it down and stole the lens. In 1871, a hurricane severely damaged the main tower and then in 1886, the Charleston Earthquake cracked the brickwork. My chapter on Tybee Island light was a reflection on resilience and as I typed my words and prepared to email them to Diane, I thought of Ellen as she fought unexpected high winds during the heat she would ultimately lose and miss the opportunity for a medal. Her face, grim and fixed with determination, rigid as steel, lingered in my memory.

*

Ellen was speaking with one of her teammates when I arrived. I had been abandoned at the door and stood around, experiencing the uncertain awkwardness of a teenager at a party. Her teammate was tall and clean cut. He reminded me of a Perry Ellis advert. Ellen was nodding and smiling, but her body language told me she wanted to get away from him. She made a sweeping glance around the room and our eyes met for an instant. I became disconcerted, I knew her, but she looked right through me as if I wasn't there. I thought it an apt metaphor. I walked towards her, but almost as soon as I'd taken my first step she caught sight of her mother, called her name, and beckoned her over. I joined them shortly after. For a tiny instant, the room grew airless.

'I read one of your books,' said Ellen.

'Did you like it?'

We shared about five minutes of small talk before she had to go. She was apologetic, I told her it was no problem, I understood the situation. I told her I was proud of her achievement. She smiled. I didn't see her for some time after.

I left Brazil the next day. There was no point in hanging around. When I got home, I had an awkward and brief chat with my wife and within a week, I had moved out and gone to our summer home on Long Island. A week later, for no particular reason, I decided to drive to the tip of the island. I stayed there for the entire day, mostly sitting in my car mulling the thoughts bouncing around my mind like lottery balls.

As the sun began to sink and hues of orange and purple and blue blended into the soft dusk, a sudden and powerful beam of light lit up the entire place. I turned reflexively, expecting to see a car, but the light was brighter than a car's headlights. I stepped out of my vehicle. I had to shield my eyes. I looked at the lighthouse which sat on a headland to my left. As I watched it sweep along the coastline and out into the blue-black sea, my phone beeped. I ignored it, the moment was too perfect to be spoiled by the intrusion of technology. I don't know how long I watched the light, but somewhere in there my thoughts came together with a kind of clarity I'd not had in a long time.

When I got home, I turned out my pockets and remembered how my phone had beeped during my lighthouse reverie. I didn't recognise the number, but I read the message.

*Sorry we couldn't speak longer, maybe we could do something before I go to France? Ellen.*

My immediate reaction was to chuckle. How unlike we were, I thought. I was from a generation who liked to telephone, she was the opposite. I thought about calling her, but I reckoned it was best if things were done on her terms.

*Of course, I'm free any time.*

A few minutes later, she replied.

*Cool. See you soon.*

A month later, she left for Europe and two weeks after I received word that there'd been an accident. I didn't get all the details. Every time I tried to find out the truth, I was rebuffed by lawyers. Finally, a man in a dark suit knocked on my door and told me the matter could be resolved the hard way or the easy way.

'I want to know what happened,' I said.

I don't know what happened in his mind, but before leaving, he explained the events of Ellen's death.

She had been whitewater kayaking on the Asli River in Norway when she lost control of her craft and hit a boulder. She banged her head but managed to regain control and get to safety. That evening, she complained of a headache and went to bed. She never woke up. I asked a doctor I knew what had happened. He told me it was likely an epidural hematoma. I only asked because I needed a name for what had killed my daughter. The man in the dark suit didn't know its name.

*

Before Ellen left for Europe, I met her in New York. We had lunch together in a small mom-and-pop bistro in Tribeca. It was one of the city's best kept secrets, and Ellen appreciated the cosy simplicity. The owner, a burly, Italian named Faustino, entertained us with his flamboyance and humour. His avuncular charm, as he moved among his customers attending to every detail no matter how small, gave the room energy. He laughed and joked and frowned and pretended to be annoyed before beaming broadly and pinching a child's cheek or scuffing up their hair.

Ellen was entranced.

'It's like being at a play,' she said.

'You should see his evening show,' I said.

Afterward, we took a stroll through Battery Park before stopping at the water where we could see Ellis Island. I told Ellen about the European immigrants who passed through on their way to a new life.

'They would see The Statue of Liberty first,' said Ellen.

'Probably,' I said.

'It's a lie.'

'What do you mean?' I asked.

'Liberty,' she said, 'they were promised liberty, but they didn't get it.'

'What did they get?'

'I don't know, but I bet it wasn't what they thought it would be.'

'You've done alright,' I said.

She pulled a stray strand of hair from her face. The wind had picked up a little, and carried on it were the voices of those who had crossed the ocean in the hope of catching the sun before it sank.

'Have I?'

Her words weren't those of someone who had been within a few hundredths of a second of an Olympic medal. They were weightless, as if brought on sunbeams infused with a breathy sadness.

'A life I did not choose, chose me,' she said.

I wondered how many others had felt the same as they stepped through the door at Ellis Island, and of how they had been robbed of the decision to determine their own future and how they had been left with only the fear of things not turning out right.

*

*Somewhere off the west coast of Africa or maybe Guyana, the seed of a storm is building, but for now, the sea is warm and rolls gently in its own wake. The fixed beam from St. Augustine light-*

*house thrusts into the salt run flowing from the Matanzas river and across Anastasia State Park to the Atlantic, where I push my boat through the sea's rhythmic rise and fall. My pilot light casts yellow ridges onto the wavetops, but it is little more than a spark in the thick dark. I look towards the land where the ridge of the coast meets the horizon's phosphorescent meridian. It looks like a hairline scar. I imagine prying it open and catching a glimpse of the day now gone.*

*The lightkeeper told me it was foolish to go out on the ocean at this late hour. He told me there were sharks, but the currents were more dangerous. He said they could take me away from the shore and into the open sea. I told him if he kept the light on me, I'd be fine.*

*'Many's a ship has gone down in these waters.'*

*'What kind of light cycle do you use?' I said.*

*'Depends on the time of year, occulting mostly on a fifty-three to seven cycle, but I can keep her fixed on you for a time if you want.'*

*'Can you lengthen the dark phase?' I said.*

*During the light's occulting phase, I turn to the open sea and strain my eyes into its vast veil of darkness. I hope if I stare long enough, a kind of sense will come to my eyes.*

*I hope it is as clear as the sheet ice on a northern lake in December, so I may see the rivers of Europe moving serpent-like into the land masses of France and Spain as if being chased by an unseen terror. I hope to see them push headlong through meadows and farmland and forests and mountains as they burrow deeper and deeper into the earth.*

*Now I imagine them rising out of the earth towards the roof of the world in great plumes before reversing their flow and cascading downwards into the waterfalls of Sweden and Finland and Norway like a girl on a summer morning bent over, hanging her hair out to dry in the sun.*

# SUKIE IN THE GRAVEYARD

Between the July heat and Jamie's relentless moaning, things were beginning to be a little hard to bear. As we drove the ten miles or so from our Airbnb to the cemetery, I tried to ignore his whining as best I could. I asked Jamie questions to distract him, but he just kept complaining, and the temperature kept rising. The air conditioning on full icy blast was barely more than a breeze caressing a scorched earth and when Jamie pulled down the window for the third time and the searing Georgia air filled the car and sucked out the accumulated coolness, I yelled at him, making him jump. He wound up the window of the cramped rental car and sat back, forcibly pushing his feet into the back of my chair.

'Stop it,' I said, 'I won't tell you again.'

'It's too hot, I can't breathe in here,' he sulked.

'There's nothing I can do about it,' I said, 'it's not far to go, so just put up and shut up, please.'

'Why couldn't we stay back at the apartment?'

'Because we're on holidays, and you need to see the outside world, there's more to life than computer games.'

Jamie didn't respond. I had the upper hand. I could sense he was formulating a counterargument.

'It's not like anyone else wanted to do anything today,' he said finally.

I chose to ignore his comment, knowing full well he'd start accusing me of making all the decisions and of hijacking what was supposed to be a rest day.

'Who wants to see a load of dead people anyway?'

Evie, who would normally stay out of any argument between Jamie and me, waded in with calm words.

'Once we get to Bonaventure, we can get a coke or an ice-cream, okay?'

'Your dad really wants to see this place,' she continued, 'it's important to him. Remember, he does plenty of things for you.'

Evie had a knack for striking the right tone at the right moment. Whether Jamie was satisfied with her suggestion, I couldn't tell, but he went quiet, and, in the moment, it was more than enough.

'What's Bonaventure?' asked Sukie who'd been sitting quietly in the backseat alongside her brother.

'It's a cemetery,' I said, 'a place where they bury dead people.'

'Like grammy,' said Sukie.

'Like grammy,' I echoed.

'I know what a cemetery is,' said Jamie petulantly, 'I'm twelve. I do know things, why do we have to hear about it all the time?'

I shared a glance with Evie. She smiled gently and squeezed my hand.

The rest of the journey passed in relative silence. Occasionally, I could hear Sukie babbling to herself in the way young children do. I could only hear one side of her conversation and felt such a glow of love for her. She was the best, nothing fazed her. After a few minutes, the car became calmer if not cooler and I could feel Jamie's resentment subside. Sometimes, as I glanced in the rearview mirror, I would catch a glance of his eyes burning holes in the back of my head. Sukie had moved right beside him, but he either didn't notice or it didn't bother him. Either way, I was pleased to see the two of them so close.

We arrived shortly after two. The drive from the Airbnb took no more than thirty, maybe thirty-five minutes, but with the argu-

The Occulting Light

ing and the relentless energy-sapping heat it felt as if we'd been travelling for longer. Once parked, we stepped from the sticky car into the afternoon's thick humidity. The air was like inhaling wet paper, and I felt sweat trickle down my back. Evie and Jamie made their way to an ancient vending machine which stood squat in the shade by the restrooms. I mopped my brow and fanned my shirt to create a draught. We were all suffering in the thick heat. Only Sukie was coping with it. She smiled and squinted in the bright sunshine.

'Are there kids in here?' she asked me, pointing to the entrance.

'It's a really big place,' I said, 'I bet there are. Do you want to go and see?'

She nodded and scrunched up her nose before scratching it.

Evie returned with a can of diet coke and handed it to me. I opened it and handed it to Sukie, but she shook her head and made her way towards Jamie, who was leaning languidly on one of the impressive pillars marking the entrance to the cemetery.

'Feeling better?' I asked.

He grunted and, after finishing his coke with an audible slurp, followed us in. I saw a scarlet cardinal perched atop a statue. It moved its head in the jerky motion birds make and flew off before I could point it out.

Like many tourists who sought out Bonaventure, I'd read John Berendt's *Midnight in the Garden of Good and Evil* and wanted to see the Bird Girl statue. It was only later, as I was leaving, a local walking her dog informed me the statue had been moved to Telfair Academy in Savannah. The book, a curious mix of non-fiction and fiction, related tales of Savannah's seedy belly and high society. Berendt wove local folklore into the narrative, creating a rich, evocative tapestry. It was this texture of ghosts and secrets and antebellum southern gothic which captured my imagination in the way only a compelling mix of fact and fable can.

The cemetery was on the site of a plantation, and one of the many stories which made up its reputation for mystery and lore told of a fire at the main house during the 1770s. The blaze oc-

199

curred during a dinner party and the host, rather than stopping the party, ordered the servants to take it outside where the assembled guests revelled late into the night by the light of the raging fire. According to the locals, if you listen carefully on still nights, you can hear the party carried on the soft breeze drifting in from the Wilmington River. There's no solid evidence to support this as fact, but never let the truth get in the way of a good story, or so the saying goes. Stories about ghosts are as much about the person who listens to them as the one who tells them. It never fails to interest me how hauntings are only experienced by those receptive to them.

Sukie was making headway along the main avenue, and lagging behind like melancholy dray horses were Evie and Jamie. They were pausing to take regular sips from the now warm bottle of water we'd brought with us. The cokes were long gone. I hurried ahead, leaving them to their heat-weary ambling, in an effort to catch up with Sukie. I heard Jamie moan about the heat for what must have been the hundredth time that day. Evie pulled him close to her and gave me a signal to hurry up and see what I could, as we'd probably have to leave before too long. I understood Jamie's discomfort and boredom, and reproached myself for not being more insistent about coming alone. I'd suggested it, but Jamie, happy in the soothing cool of an air-conditioned hotel room, had agreed to come along. I'd sold the trip on the pretext of spooky graves and ghosts and ice-cream, so I'd only myself to blame. Five minutes into the journey and Jamie's enthusiasm evaporated in the car's stifling greenhouse.

What struck me about the cemetery, aside from the pounding heat, was the serene atmosphere. There was a keenly felt tranquillity to the place which enhanced every aspect of the experience. The definition on the faces of the strikingly realistic statues, the stately mausoleums and the vividness of the ivy snaking up the ornate crypts like verdant tattoos gave the place a sense of life. It was surreal and difficult to articulate. This was a place existing in the space between both words and worlds.

Evie stopped to admire the pink azaleas clustering along the path and dotting the graves like flashes of paint in a watercolour. Jamie looked up at the live oaks, which were draped with fluttering beards of Spanish Moss.

'Why does it grow on them like that?' he asked, 'it's like the tree has hair or something.'

I had asked someone the same question as I walked through Colonial Park Cemetery two days before, and now repeated what they told me.

'It's not part of the tree, it's a separate plant that likes hanging on the branches.'

'Like a lazy leopard,' said Jamie.

I nodded in appreciation of his words.

'I think it's cool,' said Jamie, 'it makes the place seem relaxed.'

'So, this wasn't a waste of time?' I said.

Jamie didn't say anything, but I knew I'd got through to him. He moved over to Evie and felt along her arms to her hands, searching for the water bottle. He took it from her hand and twisted the top and offered it to me. I shook my head and looked up along the path to where I could see Sukie moving through the light and shadows like a butterfly. After the brief pause, we ambled along in a quiet procession, and I took in the angels and cherubs and names on the graves. I reflected on the lives those named had lived, and how they were now reduced to letters and numbers carved into marble. We stopped at a family plot and noted with sombre respect the grave of an infant. As we moved further into the environs under the canopy of tangled oaks, we noticed with increasing frequency the number of graves belonging to children. Evie moved in beside me and took my hand casually, squeezing it as she had done in the car, before disengaging and returning to sync herself with Jamie's slow steps.

I'd lost sight of Sukie and, feeling a tinge of panic, I moved more briskly along the path. We were deep into the cemetery by now, and Evie suggested we should turn back to the car soon. I told her if she wanted to make her way back with Jamie, I'd catch up with them. Jamie looked pleased by this suggestion, and they turned foot and began their slow retreat from the withering heat. Even under the thick oaks and moss, the sun pushed suffocating air from the ground like a wave of hot oil.

I pushed ahead and within a minute saw Sukie sitting at a grave surrounded by a high and ornate wrought-iron fence. I approached slowly. Sukie was in one of her dreamlike moods where nothing in the world bothered her and, lost in her thoughts, she could wile away hours narrating the events around her. She was a free spirit in the truest sense. I'd always been simultaneously enchanted and disarmed by this quality of hers, and I waited for her to acknowledge me.

After a moment, she turned to look at me and waved and smiled.

'Hi,' I said, 'you could have got lost running off like that.'

'I knew you'd find me,' she said casually, 'you always do.'

I sat on the ground with her, and she snuggled into my body. She pointed to a statue behind the wrought-iron fence.

'It's Gracie's grave,' she said.

I saw the name *Watson* on the low wall surrounding the grave.

'There are words over there about her, but I couldn't read them all,' said Sukie, 'some of them are big and some are numbers.'

I stood up and looked through the bars of the fence and read the inscription. Little Gracie Watson had died on Good Friday in 1889, aged six.

'The same age as me,' said Sukie.

She was reading my thoughts again.

I thought it apt, albeit sad, this little girl died on Good Friday. Something about the place made me think of death not in terms of finality or even separation, but as resurrection. It was the abundance of life which did it. The trees, the flowers, the skittering of small animals and the chirping of birds seemed to render death powerless. My eyes were drawn to the lifelike and life-sized statue of Gracie. It sat at the enclosure's back end, surrounded by a muted congregation of purple azaleas. The inscription told of how the statue was carved by sculptor John Walz from a photograph. I couldn't help but admire his skill.

My eyes looked down at Sukie who was examining the gifts visitors had left for Gracie. There were small stones as a mark of respect, but there was also a hairbrush and a yoyo and small toys suitable for a little girl. Planted into the ground was a blue windmill which brought to mind the Holy Angel's plot in Glasnevin where the dead children of Dublin were buried. I thought of how these children and Gracie were connected through time and distance by the winds of the world, I thought about how the winds would race across the Atlantic to spin their windmills and sound their wind chimes. My thoughts promptly stopped in this moment of contemplation as Sukie's hand curled around my index finger.

'I hear her ghost haunts this place.'

'It says in the guide if you look at her eyes in a certain way, they follow you.'

The sound of these words broke our peace and I looked instinctively to where it had come from. A young couple in smart shorts and t-shirts stood to my left. They shared a nod and one of those half-hearted stranger smiles with me, then took out their phones and snapped a picture of Gracie's grave.

'Have a nice day,' they said as they moved along.

I looked back along the path. Evie and Jamie would be waiting.

'I'm glad we came here,' said Sukie.

'Me too.'

'Can I stay and play with Gracie?'

'Yes,' I said.

She smiled at me and gave my finger a squeeze.

'I'll see you later,' she said.

'Not if I see you first,' I replied.

She skipped into the azaleas and disappeared into the light and shadows. The scarlet cardinal I'd seen earlier descended from a nearby branch and perched on Gracie's statue. The air rippled momentarily, and I watched it before heading back. As I turned, I heard the uninhibited joy of children laughing.

It was time to let go.

I knew Sukie would be okay.

# Acknowledgements

Immeasurable thanks go to the writers who have given me advice and guidance over the years. I owe the following a debt for their kindness and their time and their willingness to support my work: Ron Wallace, Grainne Murphy, Shane Dunphy, Lyn Perry, and Sophie White.

My sincere thanks go to my editor, Mark McFaddyn and everyone at Sulis for giving this collection a home, I am deeply grateful for your patience and hard work in bringing my creative vision into the light.

Thanks in no small part go to Matthew Hickmott, Gary Quinn, and Ruth Devane, who I continually press-ganged and harangued into reading these stories, mostly in various nascent versions. Your thoughtful insights and suggestions have helped shape this collection.

A big shout-out also goes to Eoin and Sam at Shorter Stories for giving the writing community of Dublin a platform for their work. I look forward to reading from this book at one of your events.

Another shout out goes to Max, Manny and 99 at UNFTR who gave me an opportunity to write a few whimsical fan fiction pieces.

Final thanks go to Edel and Joel, the two best people I know.

# About the Author

*If you feel generous and have a couple of minutes, please leave a review online where you purchased the book. It makes a significant difference to the author. Thank you in advance.*

Robert McDermott's debut novel, *Jone$town,* was published by Riversong Books in 2021. He is a twice winner of the INOTE short story competition. This is his debut collection. He lives in Dublin with his wife, son and ebullient cocker spaniel, Alfie.

# About the Publisher

Sulis International Press publishes select fiction and nonfiction in a variety of genres under four imprints:

- Riversong Books (fiction)

- Sulis Press (general nonfiction)

- Keledei Publications (spirituality)

- Sulis Academic Press (academic works)

For more, visit the website at
https://sulisinternational.com

Subscribe to the newsletter at
https://sulisinternational.com/subscribe/

**Follow on social media**
https://www.facebook.com/SulisInternational
https://twitter.com/Sulis_Intl
https://www.pinterest.com/Sulis_Intl/
https://www.instagram.com/sulis_international/